Leabharlann Baile Munna
Ballymun Library
01-2228355

E - FEB 2

THE APPARITIONS

D1339132

Withdrawn from Stock
Dublin City Public Libraries

Sligo Tree
Catherine McWilliams

Anne Devlin

THE APPARITIONS

ARLEN
HOUSE

The Apparitions

is published in 2022 by
ARLEN HOUSE
42 Grange Abbey Road
Baldoyle
Dublin D13 A0F3
Ireland
arlenhouse@gmail.com
www.arlenhouse.ie

978–1–85132–275–6, paperback

Distributed internationally by
SYRACUSE UNIVERSITY PRESS
621 Skytop Road, Suite 110
Syracuse, NY 13244–5290
United States of America
Email: supress@syr.edu

stories © Anne Devlin, 2022

The moral right of the author has been asserted

Typesetting by Arlen House

cover paintings by Patricia Doherty
are reproduced courtesy of the artist

LOTTERY FUNDED

Contents

In classical anthropology, there's a rigid distinction between "field" and "home". Field's where you go to do your research, immersing yourself, sometimes at great personal risk, in a maelstrom of raw, unsorted happening. Home's where you go to sort and tame it: catalogue it, analyse it, transform it into something meaningful. But when the object of your study is completely interwoven with your own life and its rhythms, this distinction vanishes: where (I asked, repeatedly) does home end and field begin?

– Tom McCarthy, *Satin Island* (Vintage, 2015)

For Chris and Connal and Kyra

THE APPARITIONS

Winter Journey (The Apparitions)

One afternoon in the autumn of 2003 she would walk into a cavernous public house and sit down.

I worked here one summer in '69.

A regular was waiting. He said he remembered her. He remembered both of them. The young Irish girls behind the bar.

She is disbelieving of him: a regular for thirty-four years?

You were stout, he said. The other one was thin and nervy. Read all the time.

He could hardly know what grief drove her to that place.

You went home to go to college.

I did. Would you not want to go back?

My sister-in-law wouldn't let me. He says.

What's it got to do with your sister-in-law?

She says I've no claim on the house.

Where is back?

Galway.

Leabharlanna Poiblí Chathair Baile Átha Cliath
Dublin City Public Libraries

He asks her what she's done since that time.

I went to college, got married. Then I went to Europe. I've been travelling.

Any children?

One. Away to university.

Empty nest.

I hadn't thought of it. Yourself?

Two, and grandchildren now.

Have you always lived here?

I have. What brings you here?

She doesn't say economic eviction because by his lights she's lived the high life.

I've just moved into a flat down the road.

They talk about many things, books mostly. He's a great reader. He mentions one particular story about an alcoholic marriage. Now why did he pick that, she thinks? She gets up to go, when he says I'll walk out with you to the bus stop. They part by the red brick wall of a retirement home, one of many in the neighbourhood. He says, call in again to the pub. I go on pension day. She says, of course she will.

Strange to come back to a suburb of the Great West Road to the exact spot where she changed a tyre on the way to Germany in the winter of '76. She knows what she is doing, rewinding the days, growing back to catch herself on. She knows that love was lost because the person who made the journey was the other one – a part of herself and she didn't wholly exist then. If she could just gather up the traces of the old route she might gather in the feelings that existed then, because she knows that she cannot go on feeling nothing at all for the person she lives with.

When Beatrice comes back from the pub she sits down in the dark flat and waits for him. He comes in expecting her to have left.

She was running and running and couldn't find the door until she ran right into the room with him.

I've never been to Basel, Dag says, when she starts to talk about that winter in 1976.

I walked out on a relationship. I walked across the room to a table with two German women and asked them if they'd help me leave the man I was with. He followed me over and said I was having a breakdown.

One of them was called Renate; I can still see her face. Perhaps it is your breakdown she is having. Turned out they were lesbians. They lent me the money to get home.

Dag says nothing so she prompts him.

What about you? You promised to tell me about Klaus.

Suicide. We met at university. He was studying law, but he wanted to be an actor. He turned out to be very good. He was the son of a Protestant priest.

We would say clergyman, she corrects.

He came to Strasbourg. We shared a flat together until we were kicked out.

Why were you kicked out?

It was meant to be a temporary arrangement. Then we went to Ireland. In Dublin we did Pinter. And one night at the interval I tore into him about his performance. And he walked out; he walked right out of the theatre and disappeared. It was *The Caretaker*. I went back to Germany to run a theatre.

What happened to Dublin?

I just told you. He disappeared. And five years passed.

You went to Westphalia, was it?

Then I heard he'd moved to the area and I came under great pressure to contact him. But I never did. He wasn't reliable.

Why did you tear into him at the interval?

Because he got into bed ten pages before he should have and he had to get out again. He must have stayed in the region for as long as I was there. When I moved to Hamburg, the next thing I knew he was dead. He killed himself. Perhaps I should have called him? Didn't that happen to you?

My cousin. Jesus ... Vera. I was irritated by her. I was twenty four and very hardnosed. A Marxist. And she was this floaty woman of twenty nine coming late to university, and then she falls in love or gets involved with the most aggressive man in the university.

She had a wedding which nobody wanted to go to. But I go. In fact I give her lunch. My partner takes to his bed with a bad back. There were about six of us. The tension was ... well you could have cut it with a knife. Three months after the wedding she turns up at my door. We lived five miles from the nearest town. And no public transport on Sunday. There had been no traffic past the house.

How did you get here?

I walked, she says, and her face ...

There she was and no one had told her.

Told her what?

That his previous girlfriend had walked around with a black eye, saying he'd hit her. She got a first and moved away. Ken went after every single female in my year without success; we laughed at him, behind his back.

He said Vera was boring. And she came to me because she said he admired me. The very same day we found her a room with the Professor of Old English, whose family were very kind. My cousin was from Ardoyne but she thought she was Anna Karenina. That's literature for you. Later she got a job teaching in west London. About eighteen months after she moved, she rang me. She said she still loved him and wanted to go back. She found London very fast and it frightened her. She wanted to come home. She'd spoken to him and he said he hadn't found anyone else.

That was when I told her. Oh grow up. Of course he has someone else. He's always had someone else. There's this lynx-eyed woman on the go since the day you married.

There was a strange dry squeaking on the phone, as if a door needed lubrication. Then the line went dead. And I realised I was listening to a heart breaking.

Two years later we were packing up to go to Germany. University communities are the same the world over; from Japan to Sweden you find the same people. We gave a farewell party, the chaplain turned up, he'd had a phone call. Vera had killed herself.

Did your partner approve of you moving her away from her husband?

Yes. But it was the phone call I regret. I actually crushed her hope.

I've never spoken about Klaus before, Dag says.

And I told no one about the phone call from Vera. The flat Vera lived in was around here, in one of those streets near the Abbey. She's led me a long way.

Don't tell me you believe in ghosts?

She wants to tell him about the apparitions: on the road to the ferry when she first left. Vera was there like softly falling snow adding up to something and then dissolving; a snow woman.

She believed she had seen her at the far end of a hotel reception in Venice, answering to her name, picking up the key to a man's room.

It's the first real conversation they've had. Dag had loved Klaus; she had let her cousin die feeling unloved. She had to live with that. They were beginning to talk to each other.

Did you ever see those women again?

She nods: Renate and Ditta. They were music students who paid their fees by busking for the tourists; they said I could tag along. I stayed with them for ten months. They were headed that summer for Italy. Late September, after five weeks moving through the hill towns playing music and miming tales for the villagers, we ended up in Venice. You should have seen me. I was nut brown, all flowing hair and scarves. When I looked at myself in the mirrored shopfronts I burst out laughing. I escaped myself. I had the face I wanted at last. I was beginning to add Italian to German. Dove ... which is also the name I took. We called ourselves the people of the marionette. I don't sing or play an instrument so they put a lantern in my hand, which is how I come to be leading a crowd after Ditta and her silver flute, up to the piazza where we are holding our concert. It's a combination of classical and folk. She has a peculiar coat, a rhombus of different colours. I am dressed in a bird cloak with a hard half mask. I gather up the coins. We make a lot of money in Venice. On the last night a man stepped into a photo I was taking, and I knew him. He was my ex-partner. I did something I can't explain. I said Hi. He smiles and moves on through the crowd and disappears into a hotel at the edge of the piazza.

The next morning I persuade Ditta to go with me to his hotel: I have to know if he's recognised me. We are exotic and tolerated as we trail across the pink and grey marble lobby. No one pays us any regard and I go to the desk and ask if I might call him on the house phone. I forget for a moment which language I am in and they speak to me in fluent German.

What name? A voice asks, I say his name again.

At the same time a woman at the far end of the reception desk says my name and is handed the key to his room.

Some people start journeys with a broken heart.

Dove, don't go to his room, ok? Ditta says.

The receptionist has dialled the number and handed me the phone.

Then she disappears. The lobby is empty, Ditta waits at a distance.

Hi. Last night I took your photograph.

Hello, Beatrice. He dispenses with my advantage.

I sit down and wait for him. Ditta has left at my urging. And she's not happy. He comes towards me and he sighs. He doesn't like anything about me. I am really without funds and I know this was the root of his disaffection with me. He begins a verbal assault about my failure to earn my living, drive a car, and function in the real world. But I'm learning a language here! This sets him off again and he complains about my desire to be a perpetual student. We walk between the pillars, him and me. We're shouting and weeping, and the locals are giving us a wide birth. I can't remember anything we say, but it is awful. In the portico café in an alley in Venice he unzips his face and cries. And I do the same.

'Basta!' Ditta is suddenly walking towards me. She takes my arm and walks me out of there. I go because I'm sure I will be able to go back and finish shouting at him tomorrow. But the next day he is gone. And I go to the airlines office and try to book a flight home. An official doing the credit card checking looks at me: my face is very swollen. It's not the face I want anymore. My request is refused. Fifty pounds is all you can have. He says it very respectfully. Ditta lends me the rest.

So who went to his room?

This story isn't over. She cautions.

I am seated on the plane next to a woman who unpacks her duty free goods onto the table as if she were setting up shop. She begins to speak very quietly to me; she says she's Hungarian. I am forced to turn my attention away from the window in order to hear what she is saying, so I miss my last glimpse of the lagoon. I find instead I have in my sights a taunting array of goods I can no longer afford: a scarf I have absently lingered over in duty free is lying on the table in cellophane under an opened packet of Lucky Strike, next to 200 cigarettes of the kind I like to smoke. And also my brand of French perfume. She starts talking to me about the Hungarian uprising in '56, and her own participation in it. She has launched into the middle of a political history without any small talk or preliminaries. I have been so far away all summer that I am struggling when she gets to denouncing communist societies for the lack of freedom to travel. So I interrupt and say, you know you only have the freedom to travel if you have the money to travel.

The woman looks at me and smiles. Good argument. Now convince me of the problems of capitalism which you so despise.

I'm bewildered. I'm pretty sure I've never spoken to this woman before, so I cannot figure out when I introduced her to my thoughts on the matter. The events of the last few days have come between me and my desire to speak. Suddenly I change my mind: you know I think '56 was a tragedy, no one wanted it to happen, neither the

Soviets nor the Americans. Wasn't it sparked by a bunch of right-wing Catholics who attacked the CP headquarters and hung some party workers?

She's so angry, she gets out of her seat and moves across the aisle. When she walked through passport control in front of me a bell rang out as if a boxing match had ended.

I began to wonder how I knew all that stuff.

The hardnosed Marxist at university? he suggests.

It was something I read.

And the woman at the hotel reception in Venice?

His wife.

No, she didn't believe in ghosts, but visitations from an awareness so vast it had to be expressed; a thought so insistent it materialised.

It was the pre-Lent Carnival that triggered it, she says. In 1976.

It's called Fasching. He corrects.

Right. Adults dressed up as bears and birds, accompanied by toy-townish bands.

My partner didn't like anything about it; the truth is he didn't like me anymore. And he felt guilty but lacked the courage to tell me. She says this pointedly waiting for Dag to respond. Still he says nothing.

She knows she is going home for good this time, because she had been here before, twice. Within weeks, she goes home. Then Dag comes with her. But it isn't home for him.

He's with her until one evening, standing in a car park in the rain, when he begins to throw coins into the air with both hands. He does it twice, and with such an odd expression, tracing their trajectory as they fly and then fall. It was what her infant son looked like when he discovered that soapflakes when you threw them from a box into the air rose before they fell. The child stood in a blizzard of flakes. It's a waste, Dagmar shouted. No, it's abundance, she insisted.

She gets down in the rain in the dark to collect the fallen coins she needs for the meter. He marches off towards a painted gable. Dag! She calls after him.

'He's not coming back!' The voice beside her which has spoken is that of a young man who looks like her son. He has appeared with a map. He's not wearing a coat and the temperature is dropping.

They both stare after her departing husband.

Dag! The stranger suddenly shouts.

Dagmar stops. Turns, and glimpses the configuration. He is looking into the past. He sees mother and son united against him, ten years earlier; the beginning of his decline. He sighs deeply and walks back to face the music.

He takes the map and directs the lad to a hotel nearby.

The apparitions, she marvelled, with their ability to speak out of the silence, had not abandoned her.

They travel on the N17 to a house at the edge of the woods in the dying days of the year. She suddenly became aware of a twelve-year-old standing on a tabletop, glancing into the mirror above the fireplace on the Oldpark Avenue in 1963. She is being dressed in a cloak of leaves for a pantomime in St Mary's Hall.

The dressmaker, Auntie Maud, Vera's mother, is famed for her mother-of-the-bride outfits and costumes for the Opera House. Father, brother, husband, still interned from the last campaign, her aunt sews and remakes the days.

Twelve-year-old Beatrice stands on the tabletop, looks in the mirror and sees the bird, just as she is captured by the new music on the TV: with love from me to you. She sees that she is me, and you are in the mirror.

When she woke later her attention was caught by late afternoon light outside a lattice window high up on the wall of the room: luminous with unfallen snow. It backlit the bare irregular branches that cleaved to the house, while the regular grid of the diamond lattice made a map of routes that held her long enough to contemplate the irregular beauty below.

CORNUCOPIA

Sometime in the middle of the 1950s the goddesses arrived. There were two of them. They were a gift to my grandmother, Frances, from her younger brother, James, recently returned from Rome. One had a curved, shell-like horn at her feet, out of which tumbled fruit and flowers. The tail of the horn curved upwards, towards the flung hand of the woman who was leaning with her other elbow on a half plinth, next to a basket of wheat. Her twin, the other woman, was plainer in her adornments. While she also leaned on a half plinth, in her outstretched arm she held a scroll. They seemed to me, in their pale, unvarnished state, to represent a challenge to the gaudy saints of my grandmother's baroque Catholicism. The household had its share of statues: there was a Virgin crushing the head of a snake with bare toes on the 'tall boy' in her bedroom. When we had overnight guests, usually other relatives, I slept there on a small divan at the foot of her bed. Once, I turned over to discover the snake's jewelled eyes glinting at me in the dark. Higher up in the house, on another landing, stood the Child of Prague, like a small Velasquez Infanta with wide crimson and gold skirts. I remember my mother and father standing on a Drogheda street once, on holiday, trying to work out if they had enough money left to pay for it. It became my grandmother's favourite. On New Year's Eve she ran in and out of the front door with it in her arms, for luck. I never noticed much difference in our luck after the New Year; if anything, since grandfather's death, things got a little worse. Until the year the Roman women arrived.

The goddesses had bodies with curves rather than just fat draperies. They were placed in the parlour at first, and then quietly put away. Until exploring my aunt's out-of-bounds bedroom, I spotted them sitting in the unlit hearth, the grate banked high with empty Gallagher's blues packets. Skating boots clacked amidst blue and yellow net petticoats against the door. Auntie Kathleen was lying in late, after the Saturday Plaza. Emboldened, I asked her from the hearth. 'What is this thing at her feet? This horn?'

She spoke from the depth of her bed, rackety cough following. 'It's a Cornucopia.'

'What's a Cornucopia?'

'A Horn of Plenty.'

'Uh huh. And the scroll?'

'It's a book. Books were a different shape then.'

'When?'

'In ancient times,' she said, and added grumpily. 'Now go away and let me sleep.'

My father and aunt had a disputatious relationship. I liked drama, so I always carried the things she said to me back to him, to see how they stood up.

'What kind of book is she holding?'

'That's not a book, that's *The Rule of Law*. One goddess represents the law. And the other is agriculture. Don't forget the wheat.'

The word 'cornucopia', once you've heard it, is hard to resist. It casts a bigger spell than agriculture. He wanted me to study law because he was a baker and went to night classes. What I didn't know then was that he'd been a prisoner, and he wanted me to know my rights. But it was my grandmother in one of her more lucid moments who named the goddess with the horn.

'This is Fortuna. She's from Ostia.'

'How do you know that?'

'She's in the Vatican Museum. She has the power to give but also to take away. I don't like her much. Watch out for her.'

About the scroll woman, I was still in the dark. Until grandmother suggested. 'It's a diploma. It represents learning.'

'Aye, but in law,' my father said.

My aunt's voice contradicted him. 'Law as a goddess would have scales, and a sword.'

'That's not law, that's justice.'

In an attempt to resolve the dispute between them, the goddess remained unnamed. During this time one of the arms holding the scroll was damaged. Somebody must have broken it, maybe it was me. Someone repaired the limb, I don't remember who. Afterwards, an amber line marked the place of attachment to the elbow.

All lofty aspirations about my future were lost sight off when my mother's eldest brother came back from Canada on a visit. 'This house is too big for Frances at her time of life,' he said, glancing at me. So the pair moved into a small apartment. It was the beginning of the sixties. They proved hard to integrate either in terms of place or function. Grandmother shared her bedroom with the Virgin and the Child of Prague, while Kathleen kept the goddesses on the stainless-steel draining board in the kitchen. I returned to my parents' flat above the bakery, which promptly moved them up the housing list. My mother complained I was spoiled. I didn't like sharing a room with the younger children, and I was out of the orbit of the goddesses. They came to me after Kathleen died. The scroll she held was very much reduced; the long-curved edge was shortened and sanded to a stump in her tight grip. Her sister Fortuna remained, blooming and intact as ever. A Rastafarian carpenter made a special niche for them from some bookcases he was recycling. He placed them in the centre of the wall in a house in Shepherd's Bush. Here they were revealed to have a purpose no one had discerned before, as book ends.

She remembers them. They wore blue overalls in her dream. They looked like porters, or mental health workers from the hospital; the ones the institution used to restrain people. It was a nightmare she was glad to wake up from. She had this dream a few months before they were to move. Then, one morning, glancing over the stairwell, she saw real men in blue overalls make their way upstairs towards her. The threat they posed in the dream had become reality; the dream had prepared her for an invasion of her life by forces over which she had no control. The twins had gone away to university; an action that seemed to prompt her partner's midlife crisis. She went down two floors to pack up her own room. She was unable to finish a book. He was already in there; the boss, his job to organise the others. But here he was standing in her room with the goddess holding the cornucopia, laid flat on a small rug ready to be placed in a box. The woman, when you turned her over, had a braided crown of hair around her head and a luxurious coiled rope down her back. For the rest of her life, she will remember that image, not of the goddess lying unwittingly on the blanket, but of the man's careful examination of what he held. When she opened the box later, the cornucopia was crushed. All that remained of the female body was the braided head, which she threw away at once with the rest into the trash. The broken one alone remained. When her partner left, the house was sold to two brothers from the city. The youngest one said. 'Take the bookcases, we don't want them.' Her partner had taken out three mortgages to pay their credit card bills. The debt belonged to both of them. He had simply kept the extent of it from her. She didn't have a house to put the bookcases into.

The winter I left, the snow on the Antrim plateau was deep, having fallen for three days. In Germany the street signs are written in a gothic script which was familiar from my first Irish grammar, the umlauts and circles with tails being my speciality. I find my way to the student settlement very quickly. It's on the edge of a frozen lake. We are driving between high banks of snow on roads that seem to be centrally heated.

The mathematician who is showing us the apartment is from Ohio.

'A *putzfrau* will come in the morning with towels, sheets and keys,' he explains. 'She also cleans the kitchen and the bathroom we all share.'

A tiny Vietnamese woman is shifting a heavy pot belching steam to the kitchen window. 'Visiting professor,' he tells me. 'Our neighbour.' The Ohio student returns to his guests, and I open the door on a functional room which seems like an office with a corner alcove where my bed is tucked, in this house of exiles.

The next day I find the Institute, in a different part of town. It's a fine old house with turrets. Celia is a New Zealander who speaks German with an antipodean intonation, which to my ear makes it infinitely easier to understand. Then there's Johann who only speaks *Hochdeutsch*, which I have no ear for at all. Because it's my first day, they take me to a Weinstube for lunch; normally they would eat at the Messa. The waitress refuses to serve Johann; she'll accept halting German from foreigners, but no upper-class nonsense from him. 'His parents were diplomats,' Celia explains. 'Professor, Doctor, Frau, Eva Müller is the boss and she's married to a non-academic lawyer, so she's rich,' Celia tells me airily. 'She owns a large house with four floors, three of them are let; in fact, she's my landlord,' Celia adds. 'She fucks all the young men in the department and you have to give her all her titles, Professor, Doctor, Frau in that order.' In my head I rename her Frauprof.

Later I meet Netta and Josh, a married couple. Netta is Polish, and she tried to live in Israel but gave up because it's the desert and she prefers Europe. Josh is Austrian with very sad eyes and a voice like a cello. 'You're very ballsy to come here on your own,' she says, 'especially with such poor German.' She offers to teach me; we meet for tea and German conversation on a weekly basis. They live, the newlyweds, in the gothic part of town near the Institute where little trams hum quietly up and down the street. The coffee shops have ovens of porcelain with pastoral scenes on the tiles. The Japanese at the Institute are like me, and have chosen a modern apartment; but it is modern expensive, in contrast to modern functional. Yoshi is visiting from Kyoto with his wife Akiko, a baby and his mother-in-law; he has also brought his ancestors. He keeps them in an urn by the door shrine. It reminds me of my grandmother's votive altars, lit candles in front of the Virgin on the tallboy and the Child of Prague.

It's a comparative and international department which would explain the presence of so many foreigners, but I am really wondering if I'm ever going to meet any Germans, apart from Johann, when I meet Elsa Berg, a fiftyish blonde with gold rimmed glasses and shoulder length hair. She explains that all those donnish young English men who hover around Eva Müller are actually young Germans whose English was finished at Oxford. Elsa is from the north, and her presence in the department is a corrective to Eva Müller, who is from the south. Like revenants of both sides in the Thirty Years' War, they jointly run the department. The two women are not friends. But I also don't expect women who have reached their positions of power to be helpful or friendly to younger females. Then Elsa surprises me by being entirely supportive, even when I feel I've screwed up my first seminar.

'My energy ran out halfway through and I let three things pass,' I tell her.

'That's teaching,' she says.

One Saturday, at the end of the first month, I meet my Ohio researcher from the first night. He has a German friend, Sabina, another student. We go to a Chinese restaurant, an elaborate pavilion. I am given chopsticks.

Ohio says. 'Try to speak German.'

Sabina asks. 'Why are you here?'

'Ok. I will try chopsticks or German, but not both at the same time.'

We lapse into English. Ohio keeps stroking Sabina's arm and saying. 'Peachfuzz.'

He draws our attention to the honey gauze halo that sits on her limbs, until I have to look away.

The student settlement, like all student organisations, is a place in transition. By contrast the Institute is formal and hierarchical, and in two parts: one part is science, and the other law. The lawyers seem to be ascendant. So when a group of lawyers, who appear to run the Institute, invite me on a ski trip to the Jungfrau and Engelberg, I accept.

I have been living on a Council of Europe Fellowship. I have it for five months during which I'm expected to finish my Ph.D. The teaching allows me to subsidise my income, which means I can extend my stay.

Celia, who is not coming with us because she's not one of the skiers, explains. 'This is Eva Müller's trip. Elsa Berg doesn't ski. So if you join it, you need to make sure you have Elsa's blessing. How did you learn to ski anyway? It's all very green and wet where you come from.'

'Every weekend I go up to the nursery slopes of the Black Forest. I joined a class.'

'Where did you get the gear – the skis, the boots?'

'I bought them in a sale in London on the way.'

Celia is wide-eyed. 'You are one seriously ambitious woman.'

I have let Celia's machine-gun-delivery floor me. I have begun to do this in class as well – letting things pass. Another voice somewhere deep inside, like a child in another room, is protesting, but is too far away to be heard.

I go back to Sabina's unanswered question in the Chinese pavilion. What are you doing in this country?

Ohio tells us the subject of his thesis – something about temperance movements in Germany in the nineteenth century.

'That's not why you are here,' she says.

'No, I came here to avoid the draft. Vietnam.'

'The war is over,' she says.

'But my thesis is not.'

'I'm avoiding a war too,' I add.

'What happened to the man who drove you here?' Ohio asks.

'He has a life in another country.' He has a wife in another country.

'You aren't a scientist and you're not a lawyer. How did you get into the Institute?' she asks.

'My thesis is scientific: what constitutes a literary text?' This is usually a conversation stopper, but not with these two.

'Is that wise?' Ohio asks. 'Don't you want a bit of mystery?'

Sabina gives him a warning look and changes the subject.

March. The toughest term in my teaching is now behind me.

'How do you think you performed?' Elsa Berg asks me on the eve of my trip to the mountains.

'I did half of what I'd set out.'

'That's about right for a first time round.' She says. 'It's much easier for the rest of us; we're supported by the principle of seriality, makes it less exhausting.'

I'm wondering if I'll get a second time, or if I've made a mistake in joining the ski faction, when a horrific cable car crash in the Italian Alps that winter compounds my anxiety. I have deliberately folded away pages of *Stern* with all the photographs of crushed bodies in the snow. Netta has been using *Stern* to set me translations. Usually there are lots of stories about British Royals. They mostly involve love affairs with people in the theatre: a duke with an actress, a princess with a playwright. This time all the magazine text reveals is German prejudice about the Italians' lack of care with their ski machinery.

'The operator wasn't properly trained,' Johann explains. I allow myself to be re-assured. 'And the snow conditions are perfect,' he adds. He is regarded as the leader of the snow party.

In the hotel lobby on our first day of skiing, I find Eva Müller staring at me as if I have suddenly become visible. The usual haughty smirk has given way to a cloudier, less confident face.

'I wish I'd thought to get a new ski suit, this old thing is twenty years old,' she says.

Everyone looks at me. It's true they are tall, lean and athletic, Müller most of all, but they are all in black. They look like a bunch of deep sea divers. My mother made costumes for a living, so she taught me something very simple – look the part and you can go anywhere. Walking towards them clad in sapphire blue, a body-hugging jacket and pants, everything matching, including my hat, I'm wondering if I've overdone it. I've compensated for my lack of skill by blinding them with style. But even I know from the creature that eats my insides when I'm afraid that my advantage will not last.

Netta, with her fragile candyfloss hair, is standing at the entrance to the funicular railway in sunglasses and snow boots. She's not a skier; she's come to take in the views. She hands me a tube of cream.

'Don't get burnt at the top.'

At dinner on the previous evening, while the Swiss waiters were being given a blasting by Eva Müller for handing out menus to the women with prices withheld, I asked Netta why lawyers were so important at a scientific Institute.

'They are patent lawyers. They have to determine what part of an idea or discovery is owned by the scientist and what by the corporation.'

'Are you a patent lawyer?'

'No, I'm an art historian.'

I'm halfway up the slope before I think to question this further. I recall that she doesn't have to share an office. She's going to the sun terrace at the first station to sit in a deckchair with a blanket.

The skiers pair off to the lifts which will take them to the top of the glacier. It is when we reach the third and final station, travelling up the face of the Jungfrau, that Johann, who is accompanying Eva, suddenly looks over and asks. 'What level are you? This is a black route only.'

My moment of truth has arrived. The tight panels of my suit are holding me in at the sides. 'I'm a beginner.'

'You should have got off at the last station.'

'I'll get a cable car down and meet you at station two.'

'There is no cable car down,' he says. 'We shouldn't have let you come up so high.'

Outside on the glacier, Johann begins to allocate places. The safest place on the whole route is next to the leader. 'You will have to ski in my tracks,' he says. Then he turns to Eva, who is a very experienced black route skier. 'Will you go third? Then if she gets into trouble you can lead the line.' Yoshi follows Eva, who is followed by a trio of young lawyers who are her constant companions at work.

Out on the frozen concrete of the mountain, an American woman is swearing and slamming her skis together. Finally she hurls them and screams at them. 'Mud Fucker.' We make our first traverse past her. I am deep in Johann's tracks and skiing across the face of the glacier. The first relentless traverses are fine, and the skis bite into the mountain. Then we hit the ice field and it's like skiing on marbles. Everyone loses control, but I make it because I have locked on Johann's ski path. Eva takes a very bad roll across down the field and we lose sight of her. Later, when we have all skied around an overhanging boulder, which takes us to the very edge of the glacier, Eva crashes above our heads onto Johann's shoulders.

We reach the second station with relief and, unobserved, I steady the tremor in my limbs. I am not the only one having to struggle with the body's rebellion. It took enormous concentration and skill to lead us out of the ice field. The designated routes have become icy with congested traffic, so we ski off-piste into the deep powder snow of the woods. And in this way we travel for an hour, through the darkling afternoon, flitting in cushioning silence towards Engelberg.

That evening we went to an inn that specialised in fondue. Netta is puzzled by the mood of the ski party. We raised our glasses through entwined arms.

'You may say "*du*" to me,' Eva says to Johann.

'You may say "*du*" to me,' Johann says to me.

'Do to me,' I echo.

'You do something to me,' Josh sings to Netta.

Johann's conquest of our hearts was evident as I watch Eva tilt her head back and stretch her neck towards him.

'And this,' he says, holding up the heated cheese on a fork, 'is called the nun, and this is the best bit.'

'I recover stolen paintings,' Netta volunteers. 'They are hidden as fakes. You could help me. You have great eyes.'

'I couldn't. My eye and my brain don't know each other.'

I do know I will not finish my Ph.D. That Elsa Berg will not extend my stay. And neither will Eva Müller. And I have risked all this, to have sex with Johann.

When I return from the mountains, Ohio has already moved to Sweden, Sabina must have gone too. A group of strangers are living in the student settlement.

I get up from the table to find the loo. The wine is having an effect.

'Who took my cup?' I ask when I come back.

The faces at the table smile, and resume their conversation. I am speaking a foreign language. My friends have gone. My insides plunge like a lift losing power and falling to the basement. My ears are full of noise. I am petrified by the volume of the crash when it comes, and it comes. I am gone for twenty years.

The lawyers lived their lives in such conformity; they knew all the rules, so they were always on the alert for places without any, like off-piste skiing. It wasn't simply dangerous thrill-seeking; they were looking for the uncharted, something off the map. It wasn't an escape. It was a confrontation. What they wanted was to test their courage for liberty. I wanted to escape. It was peace I was seeking, though it looked like liberty at the time. This would put me on a road that would bring me to that moment in a room in Shepherd's Bush when the carelessly held cornucopia lay in a blanket, unwittingly waiting to be dropped. That man with his little bullet head and his close cropped hair bent over her. After the house is sold, she wakes with a throat of fire, in her temporary rooms; something has fallen during the night. Silver flakes have skied across the carpet. A mirror propped against the fireplace has fallen over into the hearth, tumbling the surviving goddess, whose limb has become detached again. Up close, it looked as if she was holding the phallus in her tight grip. It was an earlier version of the virgin crushing the snake's head with her toes. I broke my arm twice; I had forgotten. Once I fell down on a road when I went back to live with them. My father took me on the night bus to the hospital to have it set; all summer I wore it in a sling. I fell again under an ambush of stones, on the road during a civil rights march, on the same arm –

detached again by the fall. The limb carried the weight of our projections. Isolated on the desk it looks, for all the world, like a reminder to give someone a hand job. Somebody once said you have to be ruined twice. The mirror in which I look is very unforgiving. I had not escaped the pattern after all.

In the few weeks before I leave London, I am invited to a screening. An actor I once had a crush on is across the room. He told me he left Wales because he used to open doors to rooms where he found his aunts weeping behind the debris of objects that piled up and kept them from leaving. I have him down as another liberty seeker. I have a great desire to cross the room to speak to him. But the self is so receded and the distance to the world so vast that the effort defeats me. I glance away, over my shoulder. That's when I see them, sitting on the window ledge, looking in: the goddesses. Ten times the size. We are five floors up in Piccadilly. I get out of the chair in which I have been sitting and move across the room.

To celebrate my fiftieth birthday, the Italian baker in our neighbourhood made the cake. It was iced with a cornucopia. He placed sprays of real berries among the marzipan fruit and flowerheads. Two days before the baker delivered this cake, the planes went into the Twin Towers. I went ahead with the party.

On the day everyone came, solemnly ate the cake and left early, and all at once by the basement door. A bell clanging in the distance from Milton's church, never audible before, called time in the house; stacked cake plates clacked in response. A small blue and yellow mayfly made of plastic glass and wire, a township souvenir, tumbles from the London window onto an Ardoyne sill, through the Alpine light of the darkling year.

THE TRANSIT OF MERCURY

My grandmother, Frances Bernard, was educated by French nuns in a convent in Lancashire, when she defeated all expectations by refusing the veil and running away with my grandfather, Charlie Moore. He was a tenor with a light opera company. This is my mother's version of what happened. There is a wedding photo from 1913 of bride and groom in the garden of the family home. Her brother, great uncle James, is standing behind his older sister and her new husband, Charlie; no sign of the parents. James was removed from school the following year when the Great War broke out. He was sent to the trenches and came home deaf from the bombardment. My mother, Maisie, never gets tired of saying that the grandparents felt so guilty about his disability they left him everything they owned – two houses, a field, and the business – while they left their only daughter, Frances, a chest of drawers, to keep her nine children in.

There was an old woman who lived in a shoe. That's me, she once remarked at an illustration of children climbing the bootlaces and hanging from an eyelet.

'The family house was supposed to come to us. It was promised.' Maisie insists. There are indeed photos of Frances Moore and her children, grown up, some in uniform, in the garden overlooking the sea in Cushendall as late as 1941. But when the will was read in 1944 the promised haven evaporated. Why did my great-grandparents change their mind about the promise to my grandmother?

'They lied.' My mother says. 'She was supposed to take the veil. So they met her deception with their own. Imagine, going to your maker with that on your conscience, lying to your only daughter. Och, the granny Bernard was alright,' my mother relents, 'but he used to wear a panama hat and lie out in the garden on a hammock puffing on a cigar. He was an awful oul rip! My father, Charlie, gave up his career as an opera singer to work for him. They sent him off on trips to the south of France and Spain to meet fruit and vegetable growers!'

We aren't talking turnips and potatoes obviously. I would not dare suggest to my mother that Charlie Moore might have given up his career to feed his nine children, especially since I took to the boards myself. Though I have since had cause to be grateful to the chest of drawers Francis Bernard left to me. I was always on the move so, Maisie said she would keep it until I got a place. The chest remained on the top landing of her house when 30 years later I returned. The rooms I now occupy are on either side of it. A more romantic person might be tempted to suggest that this reliquary had housed the power to call me home. But that would be delusional: instead something very mundane had happened. Illness, and my mother's old age, had resulted in my return. The power it held for me was of a different order.

The chest is of highly-polished African walnut with little brass handles. Only the top two drawers were ever locked. In one Frances kept her war relics: a hand-painted linen hankie edged with Belgian lace, which depicted the burning of Ypres. Yellow, orange and red flames leapt from the roof of the cathedral; one of the men in James' unit was a painter. In the other, she kept blue airmail letters, her black writing case and the red memorandums, of which there were four.

This is the power the chest holds, the memory of her practice of writing. She hadn't made the effort to compose her thoughts every day; her composition was more of a travel journal. I remember in particular a sentence:

Bougainvillea made a garland for the stone balustrade on the staircase to the grandmaster's apartments where we made our way in the afternoon.

Another time she read:

They made the sea journey with their delft packed in tea chests full of barley which lasted the length of the voyage and sustained them long after they arrived ...

But whether she made the journey, or gleaned the descriptions from her husband's trips, I couldn't say. And I expected to find the red memorandums when she died, but when the drawers were unlocked, they were found to be empty.

Still I had set out with those two sentences from her notebook and I could not erase them.

Perhaps what she wanted in reading to me, was to give me a safer identity than the one implied by my name, Flora MacDonald, or my father's marked preference for scientific materialism: flat earther was the worst thing he could say about anyone. Between them I wove an inheritance of sorts.

So it happened I bought myself a blue notebook, and wrote at the top of the page one word:

Heirlooms.

1976. They had joined a tour of the fort and when it ended, separated from the others. A lean and tanned woman waved at them to come up. She felt relieved to find herself included in the wide-lipped smile.

Half an hour later Captain Brennan appeared, white peaked cap first, until he was in full view, khaki shorts and long socks rising from the stone steps. They were sitting where Leonora had placed them waiting for him, on fan-shaped chairs facing the top of a wide stone staircase.

We have visitors for lunch, Leonora announced. She might have been describing the menu. Visitors. Yum.

On the way to this scented terrace they passed through the stone frigate's dungeons. Along the outside wall of the inner yard was an open cell on the wall of which a prisoner had inscribed his name. The cell was an open dungeon with an iron grill above it. A prisoner would have been out in all weathers. He used his fingernails to carve his name in the stone. She didn't believe the guide's information, so got down to have a look. The name was of one of the grandmasters who had fallen from favour. His nails must have been very tough. But then she also noticed how quickly her own nails grew in this climate.

Leonora has promised them a tour of the private apartment. 'Lord knows when anyone will get a chance to see the Knight's quarters again.' She and the Captain are due to hand over the fort quite soon. Their belongings are in packing cases, on the corridors.

> *They made the sea journey with their delft packed in tea chests full of barley which lasted the length of the voyage and sustained them long after they arrived ... on the island.*

Because of the dense heat, the dazzling light and the canopy afforded by vast and luxuriant greenery, the rooms seem to flow inside and out again; a fig tree in a stone pot, and here and there, pink oleander trees. They move to the small turreted alcove where they are to lunch. She is given a seat facing the sea, another little turret with a stone eye is in her line of vision, lower down and jutting out over the Mediterranean. The table is set for four. A white liveried servant stands beside.

She will wait to see if the cut glass bowls with pieces of lemon are for washing the fruit or her fingers. She is sure that what she must not do is drink from it. The glass she has carried to the table has lime and something herbal, and a little oily, thirst quenching, nonetheless. The problem is, she is presented with everything first. At some stage she is offered fruit to accompany cheese. She doesn't eat cheese. So she takes a peach, and on impulse dips it into the water bowl; resolving the issue by washing both the peach and her fingers at the same time.

How dare you! Leonora is screaming.

Captain Brennan blankly ignores his wife. Julius, who is next to her, glances into the middle of the table. The moment to have invited them to the opening has drowned. She sinks with it.

The servant steps forward to be shouted at.

How many times have I told you! You get bread for lunch whether we have guests or not.

She had never seen such a perfectly-trained human being; he was faultless in his acceptance of the rebuke. She had entered a world where the person of the lowest status takes the blame. She looked at the captain, and wondered how many people suffered for his mistakes.

Earlier, on the way here from the launch, she witnessed a curious little ceremony at the waterside: a small flotilla arriving with all the oars upright and under a fluttering sun canopy, in the bleached sunlight, a single row of white caps and navy jackets. Was this choreographed chorus for Captain Brennan? *The King and I* she thought. Whistle a happy tune. The tourist launch took them to another side of the rock to disembark so she never got close enough to see who was being received with such ceremonial glamour.

Julius loved drama. That was why he had brought her along. The youngest member of the cast of *Hamlet* on tour, he wanted her to observe and learn. You cannot play nobility in Shakespeare if you move like a kitchen maid. Observe how people behave in proximity to power. She was the understudy, but a stomach bug was causing havoc with Ophelia's rehearsals.

You are the betrothed of the prince of Denmark why are you so timid?

He was getting her up to scratch.

I was twenty when I first came to this island, he said. *I was the first gravedigger in* Hamlet. *It was a British Council tour of the Mediterranean beginning in Valetta. 1935. Some of the others on that trip went on to become greats in the theatre – Tony, Peggy, Ralph.*

He has impressed them with his name-dropping.

The Malta Opera House was full to the brim with hoi polloi. The First Sea Lord was there. The top brass of the fleet in the med turned out. It was the cultural highlight of the year.

He turns to me. *You've been to Covent Garden, haven't you?*

I have, my grandmother took me. Fokine. Scheherazade. I was ten.

I have an immediate glimpse of a unicorn directly in my line of vison, as I remember this. And a navy and gold passport issued for my current tour with the same crest.

Well, you will have some idea of the interior; the building was designed by the same fellow. I did my early training there before the tour. Hauling on ropes mostly.

He turns to Leonora and says. *If you can imagine what my perspective was. We didn't walk onto the stage, we were already in the grave when the curtain went up after the interval. So we popped up from below stage. The massed ranks of the Malta Opera House are around me. I suddenly became aware that something was wrong. I couldn't resist turning around to look: all I could see was light glinting off the tiaras.*

We wait.

Then it came to me; there weren't any men in the audience. The entire company had left.

Why?

Mussolini had invaded Abyssinia in the interval.

So the men were called up to fight the Italians? My ignorance provokes derision.

Ach. They cleared the way for the Italians, Captain Brennan says.

The fleet was withdrawn, our ship among them, I didn't get home for ten years, Julius says.

So how did you get off the island?

Fishing boat. We all split up. I went to Italy, spent the war there. It was where I met my wife.

What did you do in Italy, Julius?

I was handed a camera and told to record our progress. The 6th Army were so speedy they often arrived before the camera. I had to get them to restage their arrival.

And they obeyed you?

Of course. That's when I knew I could be a director.

Did you ever go back to the Malta Opera House?

It didn't survive the war.

Captain Brennan adds, *and they never rebuilt it.*

Well they won't now, Julius says. *Mintoff has other fish to fry.*

You do know the Chinese are building a chocolate factory in Marsaslyox, Leonora says. *Can you imagine?*

The sun was high now and the heat intense. Julius delivered his invite to the opening night. They were discussing where the Brennan's might retire, since Leonora was Belgian French and he was from Cork, when they withdrew to the salon for coffee. Flora is the last to enter, reluctant to leave the lush vegetation of the terraces. The grandmaster's apartment had a vaulted ceiling like a small basilica, cool and pristine in calm sandstone.

A tray of tiny white cups is next to a jug of coffee. The rebuked servant was nowhere to be seen. They sat in an arrangement on low chairs into which intruded a catwalk of glass showcases of garments worn by the knights. She might have expected to find suits of armour, but instead the glass cases contained priest's vestments, disconcertingly for very tall men. And the colours were unfamiliar – that rose chasuble seemed a shade too carnal for a priest.

Kiss starved, I had stopped going to mass at 15 – slipped off with a group of young men to the glens for a picnic and came back to listen to Country Joe and the Fish in a flat on the Beersbridge Road.

One two three, what are we fighting for?
Don't ask me I don't give a damn.
Next stop is Vietnam.

Actors she thinks, here I am with the *hoi polloi* in the grandmaster's salon, and tomorrow I would return to the street.

She turns to Julius. Silver haired, broad chested, a shaggy bear of a man, still attractive to women.

I thought the Knights were soldiers?

They were also priests, Leonora says.

This is not the company she thought she was in.

And its five six seven, open up the pearly gates.
Well there ain't no time to wonder why.
Whoopee we're all goin a die.

They had given her gin and tonic. She never had gin before. She thought it was delicious.

In the courtyard later they passed the rosy purple bracts of fallen bougainvillea floating on the surface of the fountain. She ended pinning bougainvillea onto the sleeves of her gown; the final costume change for her performance of Ophelia before the original actress recovered.

Later, on that momentous day, she ended also pinning down the three corners of the room, which rose to meet her in succession. Only the fourth corner remained where it was, because she was lying in it. Everyone said Julius would fire her. But instead he said, I think you might be a writer.

2016. The drawer sticks, as I push it shut, until I remember Frances Bernard. My grandmother, standing in the dark bay, becalmed in her widow's vigil, inhaling the dust of cotton lace, staring at nothing. I watched her often; the face she never showed in the bright living room; it was the face I picked for Ophelia.

There were lemon trees at the window where I washed my hands and face. I could reach out and touch them in the morning at the house. Bougainvillea made a garland for the stone balustrade on the staircase to the grandmaster's apartments where we made our way in the afternoon.

In May I find myself waiting at the back of the chapel to bring my mother home from mass, when a woman leaving early touched the foot of St Anthony in much the same way as next day I touch the toe of Galileo in the black and white entrance hall of the Lanyon Building at University Square.

I walk out into the sunshine to find telescopes on the lawn; a shadow disc with a moving surface on a white card.

'What are you looking at?'

'The Transit of Mercury.' A young scientist replies in an Irish accent.

She directs me to another telescope. I see a vast red orb in front of which is a small black spot, and then another. I think I'm seeing Mercury, but I'm told they are sunspots. When I adjust my sights to where at 16.08 in the afternoon the little planet is expected to be positioned, I find the tiniest of black dots. I see Mercury, like a full stop, the end of a sentence. Something like joy fills me as I make my way to the place where I write this down.

WHEN IN '63 IT SNOWED

When in '63 it snowed, she built an igloo in front of the bay window, like a lean-to shed, and watched a doctor from the Royal go by on skis. When the house melted after five weeks she returned to school, and the trolley buses resumed their journeys past the door, on the road where once there had been ski tracks.

The holiday occurred before the entrance exams for the new school. There was a competition between her father and his sister as to which of their children would score the highest, and she knew her cousin was cleverer. When her cousin drew pictures, there were lines attached to the arrows showing where each one went. They looked like wires in the sky. She missed the snow; the memory of it sustained her. It had been a relief from persistent gloom.

It was a relief from that teacher with the stick. The one who beat her hands for ink blots. And untidy work. She never came first because her work was so messy. Her father had a friend who was a teacher in a college. He was preparing his nephew for the grammar school entrance exam; she could join them. Sunday afternoon, two buses away, the terminus at the limestone gates of the college.

And then a short walk to the new houses. Prince Edward Gardens, after the Queen's latest child. The house was so new it smelt of plaster drying. Jimmy Toms sat opposite them. His nephew Drew was wearing a school uniform, even on Sunday.

What happens, Jimmy Toms asks, *if you write a paragraph, but something else occurs to you, that belongs to the paragraph? What do you do?* She stares at him; this was exactly her problem. It was why she was being beaten. It was why she woke up screaming at night and wouldn't go to school next day. In her compositions she always thought of something later, and she'd write a new sentence in the margin and put an arrow next to it, linking it to the space on the page where it ought to go. He waits and then says. *Well, don't go back and revise it, but find a way to return to the subject. It will surprise the examiner who will think you have finished.*

The weather changed on the third day, a thickened whiteout enveloped the valley. They moved to another lift system. This time there were no queues. The cable cars were empty taking people to the top. A weekday, most of the skiers had returned home or to work. Their party stayed close.

Johann pointed out the ski patrol on the slopes. She liked the whiteout, it slowed everyone down. The slopes weren't icy but powdery. They were mostly red routes for intermediate skiers.

A bell clanged in the mountains. 'There's a monastery nearby', Johann said. 'They make yoghurt and cheese, as well as liquors.'

She had never eaten yoghurt until that winter: mit himbeeren, mit erdbeeren, mit blaubeeren. *They would sample some for breakfast. They had moved that morning from the hotel to self-catering, since Eva and the others with tenure had to return to the Institute. She remained to take an extra holiday with Johann, Yoshi, and one of the English-speaking German researchers, Hans.*

Earlier, Johann's throaty Volkswagen drove them to their B&B on the outskirts of Engleberg, where they could stay for several days for the price of one night at the hotel. She could put off the decision about her future for as long as possible. What would she do? How would she earn her living? One thing was certain, she could not and would not return home.

She needed more time in the mountains. The effort to physically stay on her feet didn't allow her mind to wander off in search of solutions. She preferred this dense white mist to the sharpness of the ice field at the beginning of the week.

It was Johann who said Follow me and do everything I do.

When they all sweep up together, he watches her turn and says you're good.

I'm just copying you.

Yoshi laughs

That's not easy, *Johann says*. If it was easy everyone could do it.

Later a single skier in a red jacket cuts through their line and swiftly disappeared into the fog.

Who was that? *She asks when Johann halts again.*

Ski patrol, *he said*. They are letting us know they are on the mountain.

It was then a whining moaning started up, like a huge animal in pain. The sound was behind them. All heads turned in the same direction. She could not imagine what kind of animal would have the volume to cry out like that. She looked uneasily into the dense whiteout, as if waiting for an explanation from the mountain.

Avalanche, *Hans said quietly.*

Close, *said Yoshi.*

It's alright, *Johann said loftily*. It's in the next valley.

She wants to know how much the car is worth. Her partner is speaking to her. She stops writing.

I don't know, she says looking out over the office car park, and the sun on the redbrick chimney stacks.

She attends to the room – the wire cage on the window, the graffiti on the brick walls, outside; the framed film posters, his theatre awards, evidence of a career, indoors.

Tell her the registration number, she can work it out, she says.

He covers the mouthpiece of his desk phone.

Be reasonable, I can't upset these people. They are trying to help us.

I don't know. I don't even know what season I am in.

She doesn't know, he says into the phone. Then he says *yes* tersely, several times.

She knows she has spent more than the car is worth getting it ready for the journey: new tyres, a full service which required a replacement clutch; then a wing mirror was pulled off by local kids, and she had to find another fifty pounds. The young guys at the valet service asked her if she was going on holiday? They were curious because it was the end of September.

She had booked the car on the Saturday night ferry to drive Daragh to England. She is looking forward to the drive with him, she hasn't seen much of him this summer. She booked her return for Monday night. They would spend one night on the ferry, and she would spend the second night in London after she had dropped him off.

What if they try to repossess the car before Saturday? she asks later.

They won't take the car, I told her it was your car.

I was in the room with you, I didn't hear you say that.

She can see the ferry from her bedroom window at least seven months of the year. During the other months the trees are too dense. The last time she could see the lough's arrivals and departures was in May.

Aren't you taking the sat nav, he asks?

I prefer a map in my head.

I have maps on my phone, her son says, ever alert to resolving a dispute.

Daragh has so much stuff the car sinks beneath the weight of it. And she's fine, until they get to the ferry. She sees it light up in front of her like a multi-storey hotel parked at the dockside. She hadn't realised how high it was until she got up close. She moves forward. It is her turn – there is no one in front – when a crew man in a hard yellow hat beckons. As she drives towards him, he points to a long ramp running parallel at an acute angle to the height of the ship.

Deck 6, he says.

What she sees is a ski slope. Her son is texting, so he doesn't notice. She heads for the steep ramp. She begins to drive slowly upwards. The car is too heavy. *I can't, oh I can't.* She's back in the alps and winter and she's powerless. The car starts to slip back. She applies the handbrake. Her son stops texting and turns to look at her in disbelief. The guy in the hard yellow hat is beginning to walk up the gangway towards her. She looks in the rear mirror. Another car has followed her onto the ramp. She glances up ahead; the top of the slope is too far away.

You're not in first.

First? Am I not?

Not.

He is foreign, Polish, she thinks. She is aware also of her son beside her. She can feel his anxiety at her latest failure.

You need to put the car in first and apply more power, the yellow hat says.

He speaks English and he is telling her how to drive the car, confirming her high opinion of the effortless skills of foreign workers. *Apply more power.* That could be what is wrong with her life. She changes gear and applies her foot to the accelerator. Slowly the heavy car moves up the slope and then gathers speed until she arrives at the top.

On the top deck there are no more yellow hats, but a crewman in a dark jacket beckons her forward to the front of the ship. Once parked she gets out, walks to the rail, and looks down. She will find that dockworker on the journey back and thank him. Daragh was shaken but his face now mirrors her relief. How stressful a parent I am, she thinks.

The first time she felt the baby move was on this crossing. She was on her way from Liverpool. It was the middle of the afternoon. She was dozing on a bunk, and there was a rushy flow inside her, as if a fish had turned over in a bath. She found herself on the floor of the cabin. What just happened? The tannoy announced they were passing the Isle of Man. She remembers that she left the cabin and went up on deck. The afternoon sun was shining on the island when it came to her that it was the baby that had made the rushy flow. Another traveller, she thought. Likes the sea.

This time it's a night crossing. She wanted to have the day ahead to reach her destination. If she went up on deck now it would be freezing with only sharp faraway stars for company. They have shared a cabin, mother and son, because of the expense. In the morning Daragh has instructions to call her. She uses the bathroom first. When it is his turn, she gets dressed quickly. She pulls her jeans on under her nightdress, like she's at the beach. *We'll have breakfast on the road,* she tells him. His father has drawn her a map. They come off at Birkenhead. And the first stop they should make is Stafford. Liverpool is empty on Sunday morning, still and grey. Daragh had his first birthday in this city when she was in rehearsals at the theatre; where she parked in the city centre and was surrounded by small boys carrying flick knives. They offered to look after her tyres for a pound a tyre, when she had already paid to park.

By the time they reach Stafford the sun has come out. As they are pulling up at the services, he says, *I don't have any money until the grant comes through.* He is self-supporting and doesn't live with them, so she hasn't kept an eye on this. *We are not out of the woods yet,* she thinks absorbing the shock. He explains he used the last of his birthday cash from his grandmother to buy them coffee on the ferry last night.

Of course, you did. I'm so sorry, she says.

It was her mother even now who remembered to find out if he had enough cash to get by. She feels heat rising in her face at this neglect. She withdraws money from the cash point and buys them both breakfast. It's not the kind of breakfast she usually eats. They drink strong tea and eat eggs and white toast. He has fried black pudding, which is new, she thinks. Probably the new girl. Money trouble always shocked her in the gut. She shovels down food to deaden the impact. No milk and no butter for either of them. He has eaten dry toast and dry cereal from infancy; there is something he cannot tolerate. He's not like her, though, thank god, she thinks. He is very good at languages like his father. And he played several instruments at school: strings, drums, wind. He can get a sound from anything. He once told her, when he was fifteen, that string players were very neurotic, while wind players were people to make friends with. But he didn't choose to specialise in either music or languages because he loved them. Whereas she made a career out of what she had a passion for. And then refused to understand or work at anything else. Hence the lack of money skills.

When I first came to this country, it was to the Southwest.

What took you there?

Emotional reasons.

The carpenter?

The woodturner, she says. *And the eighties. Before you were born. A place to be young in even when you weren't. I cleaned cornices at the rate of a foot an hour. I invented this process: the steam from a kettle held close to the surface of the old plaster, you allow it to boil dry. Then you apply a toothbrush to the loosened wet cornice. The old gunge ran down the walls, which were made of stone and already stripped off layers of wallpaper. Sometimes a rose cornet or a grape cluster or an oak leaf would loosen, which was fine because it made painting behind it much easier; then you glued back the repainted pieces. I was so proud of that cornice. It was in the big dining room overlooking the garden. I got the fireplace at an auction, a pine fire surround; it matched the wood on the shutters. The shutters and all the doors were sent away to be dipped; beeswaxed to finish, and on all the little imperfections in the wood. It was my first big job. It was built in the time of the young queen when they still thought they were Georgian. Lofty elegance and solidity.* She says. *We bought the house for 8000 pounds and sold it to two lawyers for a small fortune.*

How much?

Fifty grand. I got away with twenty clear, after we separated. Then I moved on and bought another neglected antiquity.

Why did you stop?

The physical work never left me any energy. And I got pregnant with you. Which was all I ever wanted. Then, of course, I had to employ someone else to do the building work, and that was, well, financially reckless.

All you ever wanted was to be a writer.

I wanted both.

She doesn't want to continue telling that story from there to here, because she is returning him to England to university; and she has stalled in her own work. She makes a mental note to stop speaking in monologues.

What are you working on? she asks him.

Extinction, he says.

Could you narrow the field down, she asks.

Of the species.

Yes?

Take water quality. If you had to choose between the data the Environmental Protection Agency put out, which says the water is clean and healthy, and the fact that the mussels died. Which would you trust?

The mussels.

Why?

Because nature participates.

You always say that. The reason you trust the mussels is because they are integrating over more parameters. And you must make sense of their behaviour.

Next time she looks, he's asleep. His head is back, his mouth is open and the sun is very strong on the windscreen. She hasn't been into the library in months, where the keyboard taping sounds like rain on the roof.

On the fourth day the fog cleared. Johann drove them to another location, a different lift system, where you sat on one side of a pick-axe handle and allowed yourself to be pulled along. The presence of the skier sitting on the other side enabled you to keep your balance, while you both grabbed the handle between you. She was very confident until some young woman up ahead dropped her ski pole, and Johann ever gallant decided to get it. He was skilful enough to ski off, retrieve the ski pole and rejoin the pulley line further back. She found if she didn't move a muscle in her backside she could hang on. She kept her balance by planting her skis wide on either side of her body. Then she enjoyed the expansiveness and the solitude. The only sound the mechanism of the pulley, whirring, and the swishing bye of skis in the snow. The valley changed; the woods crept nearer; the angle of the climb changed as well. The air was colder. She looked down at the track. She was following a fiction: the early memory of tracks in the snow before the entrance for grammar school, in the winter of '63. She had to pass the exams or she would end up working in a factory or a mill. Her father and aunt drove their children forward with this mantra. She was on this mountain because she had passed her exams. And here the life-threatening enormity of the matter of existence confronted her. She had stepped out of history. The snow conditions in this place had allowed her this mobility; just as the conditions at the frozen lake in front of the student settlement where she lived allowed her to stand on a place that would not endure once the ice had melted. Suddenly she hit a rock on the track beneath her valley ski and she flipped off balance, off the ski lift, and down onto the slope and slid and slipped at a terrifying speed until she came to a rest in deep snow at the edge of the woods. She disappeared so rapidly that no one had seen her fall.

A steep ridge now stood between herself and the passing ski lift. She couldn't climb to the ridge again even if she removed her skis because there was no purchase for her boots. She was aware that she was being watched. A large deer and a fawn stood calmly regarding her intrusion. Oh stay, she thought, here. As if they had grazed the edge of her mind, the deer made a sudden movement, and sank away into the woods, like someone slipping beneath the surface of a lake. I have lost my place, she thought, glancing up the faraway slope, to the passing lines in the sky. She would have to ski out around the tree line to find her way back to the valley and society again.

He moves his suede head. She is getting used to the haircut.

We're here already? He says, blinking in surprise.

There was a toll road around the Midlands I wasn't expecting, she says. Seven years since she was last on this road, and then it was south to north.

I need your help now with the directions to your street.

Drop me at the porter's lodge and I'll get a map.

They pass the stone faces of the philosophers. Cotswold stone, she thinks, eyeing the landmark building, like the rendering on our first house. I never did like limestone.

She has wandered through the archway into the college garden while he goes to the lodge for his keys. She finds a bench and waits among the climbing roses.

I have to get a new gown in order to eat, he says, holding out the letter of appointment. High Table.

Turl Street. We'll go after lunch. She looks around the quiet bower: two white butterflies with inky edges flutter against the yellow sandstone opposite, like the torn fragments of a page.

The best house I ever lived in was with you and your dad, she tells him at lunch.

I loved that house. Why did we ever leave it? He asks. *Why weren't we the sort of people to live in one house for our whole lives?*

She's forgotten what a minefield talking to him can become. How close the wounds of their financial reverses are to the surface of every conversation. How he feels they have squandered their prosperity.

We were rackety bohemians. We lived freelance lives –

You did exactly what you wanted all your life.

What we learned was that Bohemia is a place you fall into; it's not one you aspire to. But we wouldn't have learnt that if we hadn't taken the chance.

Yeah. And then there's the shooting oneself in the foot; and all the addictions and collusion with addiction that make up a life.

She is about to defend herself when she remembers he once said, *Mum when you drink wine at dinner you become detached.* He was twelve.

I did fail, she admits. *It wasn't alcohol. It was cowardice.*

I am not accusing you of cowardice.

It was, though.

What were you afraid of?

I saw what I was facing, and I lost my nerve.

Do you think the pressure made my dad ill?

She nods. Her husband looked like a man who had parried a rockfall.

The sensitivity of complex systems, Daragh says. He is thinking about his work now. His father has always been his hero.

When they arrive in the street, she pulls up and parks with her hazard lights on. Double yellow lines everywhere. She must park as close to his place as she can because of the weight of his stuff. He gets out of the car and begins to shift the archive boxes, his gear, the big suitcases. He assembles them at the front door of his building until she can park properly. A nearby warning light gives her the opportunity as a space opens. And then a hailstorm begins as she pulls on the handbrake; she must stay in the car. He is kept in the apartment block, moving up and down the stairs with his things, while they wait for it to cease. The hail fell like rocks onto the windscreen, a collision with the iceberg of the unspoken. Sorry. To go back and say sorry to that brave twelve-year-old.

Her wing mirror, ripped off a few days before she set out by some neighbourhood kids, had been replaced by the garage, without removing the job number. LAG123 was whitewashed on the mirror. Even the valet service didn't remove it. It felt like a label. When she opens the door the whitewash is streaked, the mirror washed by hail. Everything spent.

Somewhere, in the quiet afternoon far back in a college, she can hear strings; she remembers his fiddle in her room at home, and a guitar, and a mandolin, for which he'd adapted O'Carolan's 'Farewell to Music'. Daragh is standing on St Giles, smiling in sunlight through falling leaves, when she heads off into whatever is left of the day.

It is four o'clock when they meet again at the third station, which is halfway up the slope.

What happened to you? *Johann asks.* We waited.

I couldn't find my way back.

It's too late to go up again.

She nods. I know what that means. I won't make it to the top.

Johann looks stricken. This fatalism is so defeatist.

Yoshi turns and scrutinises them. He understands from the tone of the exchange that she and Johann are already lovers. But it is Hans who takes up the challenge.

Come on, let's go!

They head out again into the packed snow, but this time they follow Hans along the route past the entrance to the middle station; it's a wide run that goes around the mountain. They never descend, but trace the tree line until they approach at speed a deep u-shaped valley run.

Don't be afraid, *he says.* Go in fast and you will have enough momentum to arrive on your feet on the other side.

He demonstrates by going first. He flies down the icy u-valley and takes the other side of the slope at such speed he lifts above the ground on the far side until he lands and travels on out of sight.

If I go down slowly I will not make it up again, is what she grasps. The momentum is what drives the ascent. She skis at speed down into the valley and rises the far side of the slope and rises again above the ridge until she spots Hans. He waves a ski stick at her and she comes down behind him, nearly toppling on the turn. It's the only uncertain bit but she lands on her feet and holds her balance. Yoshi is laughing

when he crashes in among them. Johann arrives last, tired,
and grumpy, landing heavily.

I left the earth, *she tells them.* I made a great leap.

Now there's an omen, *says Hans.*

And then it is over. The snow has gone. The pavement is under her feet, and when she looked up afterwards on her way from school, she noticed how the overhead tram lines mirrored the lost tracks in the snow.

UNDER THE WESTWAY

Have you eaten?

Not very hungry.

Are you still not?

Yes.

There's pasta.

That'll be great.

How long were you travelling? She asks.

I left at 2.15.

Five hours. It's a two-hour journey at the most.

I came off the motorway early. There was a sign saying low emissions zone, please exit. As I've an old car I just thought it meant me.

No. It's lorries. You're very suggestible.

Anyway. Then I found myself passing Ealing Hospital. And I thought, well why not go and look at the flat.

Why did you go there?

I wanted to confront it ... I needed to walk away of my own volition.

Was it negative or positive?

It was positive ... To be honest I couldn't see past the flat. I was going to get there and park and get on the tube to come here. But then I found I couldn't park anywhere. It was like a grid. The whole place since I lived here, seven, eight years ago. Even the garages said 'no parking' except at the pumps. So I drove on to find the Westway, but I had to go to the loo first and I had to find a tube station. Then I couldn't get to the loo because my Oyster card was overdrawn, and I couldn't access the station.

That's because you haven't been in London to top it up.

I couldn't find the Westway. Can you believe that? I couldn't find where I was supposed to go. I kept finding instead where I'd been. I drove past all the places where I spent the last thirty odd years; significant places.

All on the way here?

Yes. But I wasn't consciously getting lost. I was unconsciously finding and remembering where I'd been.

I agree it was deliberate. Either you deliberately didn't want to arrive here or ...?

I had to ask directions to the Westway, and this guy said, *it's up there!* Pointing at the road above my head. And I had to drive off and find the entrance.

No mean feat.

Through two sets of traffic lights and a right turn, except it says, 'No Right Turn'.

So what did you do?

No choice. I turned right.

You were disobedient, good!

So there I am, on the Westway, and I head in the direction of City of London, and all the time I think this is wrong; when low and behold the A1 and Euston show on the sign. I hit all my targets: Marylebone, Euston, Kings Cross, Caledonian Road. Islington Town Hall, Highbury, before I get lost again and stop.

I told you to look out for the cinema.

I know. I know.

You don't trust women.

I don't trust women?

Five hours to do a two-hour journey? It's mad.

I'm not mad, I'm depressed.

You're not depressed. You are stressed. I think you are in such a state of stress you gave yourself a five-hour task to distract yourself from it.

I did?

I don't think you were ever lost. I think you were on a quest. I think you don't let one side of your mind know what the other side is doing.

I'm in control of this?

Definitely.

The older woman catches sight of her own reflection in the glass door to the night garden. The worst bit was under the Westway, she says.

Why was that?

Well I worked out that you weren't going to come and rescue me.

I was working.

So I could either go back the way I came, or I could push on and find the way here myself.

And you didn't regret not using sat nav?

Oh, god no. I find that voice telling me what to do very disturbing. Especially when you can't shut her up.

The clock timer goes off, shifting about on the work surface. The older woman is startled.

What's that?

It's your pasta, the younger woman says, checking her phone: I'm seeing someone. I don't know how it's going to pan out but ... so I won't introduce you yet.

I don't want to meet anyone.

Why not?

Because I'm traumatised. You've been married to the same person for years, and a week ago I get an email saying it's over. I arrive expecting to find you in bits, and what do I find when you open the door? You look really pretty and you're grinning from ear to ear. You might at least look miserable, so I can sympathise.

It's a fallacy that if you express pain people will be moved by it. A very small number of people will be moved. Another group will add to it. Most people will not feel anything at all.

I wish you wouldn't behave as if you were assessing me.

I'm not assessing you, the younger says.

Yes you are. You've been doing it since I walked in.

I think James and I splitting up has put a lot of people under pressure to look at their own relationship.

The person I'm trying to leave is my mother. You know she jumps when I walk into the room – the worst bit is, she stares at me first. Then she jumps. I feel like saying – would you ever look in the mirror! I should be the one who jumps.

She watches as the younger woman pours half a bottle of white wine into the sink. It's sour, sorry.

She hands her guest a glass of water and places a bowl of pasta on the work surface.

What made you decide to split up?

He raised my hopes, and then I couldn't take it anymore.

The phone rings and the younger woman says, I need to take this call ... Hi, you do know if you cook a meal once a week and do some light vacuuming that will lower the rent?

The voice drifts out of ear shot. She pushes the sliding door open to the garden, to avoid her own reflection.

The worst bit was under the Westway – she pulled up at that hotel, just sat there looking, remembering she'd spent an afternoon, an adventure with someone. He ordered wine from room service, and he made the waiter stay and open it while she was lying in bed, and he kept speaking to her while standing next to the waiter. He even used her name.

You'll enjoy this wine, Rosaleen. It's got a great bouquet.

The waiter stood slowly opening the wine and looked across the room at her, lying in damp sheets.

She steps out into the garden to let the younger one go. Then she finds she cannot.

What would you do differently? she thinks.

Send the waiter away and get your man to open the bottle himself!

Next morning she found the house quiet, and in the garden room the large double-chested stainless steel fridge empty when she looked into it. A knife stood in a jar of jam on the work surface, next to a flung plastic wrapper with the end of a loaf. Nobody has any time here, she thought.

Her parking permit for the street registered fifty minutes to expiry. She worried she would get lost again. And vowed to upgrade her phone to access maps in future.

She knew she had to leave London finally and drive herself to Belfast. Seven years earlier because of the shock of all their losses, she had lost control of her limbs. She couldn't drive the car. Her brother had come to bring them back. He was the brother she didn't know; one of the people she had raised a blank screen in front of. But the blank screen had operated internally as well. She had not allowed herself to know her own mind. There were things she wouldn't allow herself to think about. But she knew when she removed the screen, it would be a mess.

The worst time was under the Westway. She felt she had come to the edge of a field where the boundary with sanity had become unstable – as it had been in the summer of '69 when she returned to find her mother clinging to the banisters; she was afraid that if she moved one degree in the wrong direction she would cease to exist.

She steadied herself for the road.

LAMP

The new house was set in an enclave, one of seven among a copse of very tall elms. Officially the site remained unnamed. The address was advertised as 'off Nelson Road.' This was the name of the street they entered the cul-de-sac from. Only when the site was complete would the street be named and a number given to the house. They had been allowed to occupy it early. In the meantime the post would be redirected from the old address to the estate agents' office, and they would deliver it or it could be collected.

Formerly, she had lived in another part of the city in an old house where her neighbours were Asian Christian and Muslim families on one side, with whom she got on; and on the other, a Turkish landlord with a penchant for chopping down trees, with whom she didn't. She had managed the tensions until her husband left and she couldn't afford the mortgage. As soon as the 'For Sale' sign went up, and a couple of buyers were intrepid enough to approach the house, a posse of white bearded elders in long gowns would materialise sitting on the wall with their backs to the garden. Her failure to sell led to her departure to Sweden for two terms, while her husband's solicitor felt more equal to the task.

In Sweden she had rented an apartment in the cobbled precincts of a small university town. Now she lived with a new mortgage, and the hum of a concrete mixer at the other end of the close, as the last three houses were rising up from the foundations. She liked the new arrangements, once the builders had gone for the day. She and the boy were alone with the birds and the elms.

One day, a few months after they had moved in, the stone jars by the front door vanished; a shadow had appeared at the glass. She had the jars from her husband's family, Connswater Distillery it said on them. It was the only time she had ever in all her travels placed them at the front door. She gathered from this that she had misjudged the neighbourhood. She retrieved a jar rolling away down the path. The only person visible was an old man shovelling sand at the building site at the far end of the close. She went back inside. An hour later, from the end of the hallway she saw the shadow again, and this time it stayed and rang the bell. The old man was back.

He was standing at the door with a can. He looked hot and much too old to be working on a building site. He asked for water to make tea. She brought him in to fill his kettle and then offered him a cup of tea. She set a tray with a cloth, cup and saucer, jug and tea pot. She sat down with him at the table by the sliding door to the garden. It was cool in the house.

He looks around the room he has helped build. He is quietly sipping tea from her good china. The bill pile on the floor by the patio door has doubled its reflection in the glass. I can afford to live here, as long as no one gets sick, she thinks. And she is keeping an eye on the time. School is out at 3.30 and she has to pick up her son. Her concentration is poor, though she is trying to inhabit this moment of calm. She is aware that he has seen her driving in and out of the entrance to the close with the boy. She noticed him this morning standing by the sand pit.

As if reading her thoughts, he says: do you just have the one?

I do.

In the middle of his tea, with his back to the patio doors, behind him a potted mimosa, he remarks: they're recruiting them off the building sites to go to Bosnia.

Her husband wooed her with mimosa.

Sorry what? Who? Recruited who off the building sites? Is that why there isn't anyone on the site today? But she finds she hasn't spoken, and her silence prompts him to add something even more puzzling.

I told my son not to go.

She nods as if she has understood. But she hasn't. This kept happening. A remark would disturb her equilibrium and she'd push it away. Like she'd pushed away the knowledge of her husband's affair. Even when it was clear he wasn't coming back, she appeared passive. She hadn't even told the boy. And she still wore her ring.

The old man is waiting for something. She wasn't good at asking questions. She didn't gather information that way. She looked at things for a long time, as if fishing for a thought. The old man is finishing his tea when she forces herself to speak: does your son work on the building site?

Yes. He got me the job.

Where is he today?

The old man sighs: in Bosnia.

She can't think of anything to say, when he adds: the army wouldn't have them. They are not good enough.

Finally, at this baffling turn of conversation, she asks: who are they?

Mercenaries.

Her mind is freezing.

Don't you watch the news? Haven't you seen the pictures from Sarajevo?

When he has gone away with his kettle of water, she still feels unable to understand the extent of his distress. Or why he has chosen her as a witness. Or why she feels so uneasy at his parting remarks: I don't know what will satisfy them when they come back. But they'll never be bricklayers again.

A fair-haired woman is waiting on the lawn in front of the schoolhouse: she is making faces at the small girls who are waving from the window. Another woman with dark half-moon eyebrows crosses the lawn towards this woman.

Manjit can't come to your birthday party, he has a music exam, the dark woman says.

Oh, what grade is he?

The women talk pleasantly behind inscrutable faces. She is glad to be outside this circle. They are both doctors, she thinks, one of them is also married to a consultant.

She doesn't like the school; it's too formal an education for the child. For both mother and son. She didn't choose it; her husband did. He is paying the school fees. She wishes she could ride up on a motorcycle with two crash helmets and take her son away, churning up the lawn and crashing through the gates. But so far, her only act of non-conformity is to turn up in a floppy velvet hat and long skirt. And play Ian Dury loudly on the car radio: *Sex & Drugs & Rock & Roll!*

How was school today?

I dunno. I dunno. Every time I walk into a room people run away crying.

Did you say something that's upset them?

I'm afraid to open my mouth.

Fuckem, she says in sympathy. Fuckem all.

Fuckem all. Fuckem all, he repeats gleefully.

A word of advice, she says to Dan. Don't say that out loud, ok? But you can think it.

The following Sunday, late June, she was sitting on the slopes of the Botanic Gardens; he was resting against her knees and they were listening to a barcarole from *The Tales of Hoffmann*; as the long bow drew back, out of the corner of her eye two arms' length away, the letters on the back of a t-shirt come into sharp focus: *the Long March from Belfast to Londonderry*.

She looks around: everything is normal in the park. As it was before she read the slogan. No one else would have seen it, or cared. Or understood. In this country it meant nothing. Only someone from home would understand. Why did she have to see it? If she were blind or short-sighted she would have been defended, safe. Her very alertness, her powers of observation, were contributing towards the snare.

The woman wearing the t-shirt was blonde with very short hair. The grassy slope around the bandstand was packed. And in the pause in the music, as a long bow began its slow movement across the face of the instrument, a peacock screamed on the grass. She gathered up her son and left the garden.

A few days later a group of men marched towards her in a broad street. She was on her way to work, it was the end of a run. Since her baby-sitting arrangement had fallen through, Dan was with her. He could sleep on the sofa in the green room if he was tired. The men were all in their twenties and were chanting. When they got close enough to pass the chant wasn't about a football team. It was about Ireland: *No Surrender to the IRA*. And there were no other people nearby, only cars passing. When they were gone, they took the sound with them. It was a strange thundery summer's evening.

She wondered if this had anything to do with the old man.

She watched the sky redden and deepen, and the temperatures soared. She became convinced that the world was ending, to believe that it was necessary to prove how good one was to qualify for being saved when the planet they lived on died. She began to believe there were lists of people to be transported to safety on another planet.

She knew Dan would qualify, but she would lose him unless she could think of one good thing she had done; and she remembered she had made a cup of tea for the old man. She went looking for him, but he had disappeared. She decided to contact her husband, so she drove to the old house. But she found a 'To Let' sign outside it. When she glanced up at the attic window, she saw a large Union Jack inside the window instead of a curtain. In what had been the child's room. Why not? This is England, she remembered. There were VE Day and VJ Day celebrations at the school. But not in this neighbourhood. There was no other flag in the street.

She decided to write down the things that were happening to her. But she became afraid when she wrote down the words. So she tore the pages up into small pieces and buried them in the flower pots in the garden. But the birds flew down and pulled the paper out of the soil. Even the birds knew. The paper, like breadcrumbs thrown on the grass to help her find her way home, would not disappear. So she gathered up the pieces of her torn mind and took them indoors to burn. The burning of the paper pieces set off smoke alarms which she could not turn off. Hours later this brought social workers to her door. Her mind had received a shock.

She had stopped watching the news years ago. Resolutely keeping it at bay, she couldn't afford to be overwhelmed by it. When she started watching again, she became aware of brown-skinned women and children on buses; of burning tourist villages in the former Yugoslavia; that the Cardinal of Westminster was critical of some recent court decision. She heard the word Tutsi. And Hutu. But didn't listen to what it was attached to. She felt she had lost enough power over her own life, and these small deviances were important to her. She took to watching *Zig and Zag*, a couple of noisy Irish puppets at breakfast time with the boy; it cheered them up before school. She received a letter from the principal criticising her for allowing Dan to watch puppets whose dialogue he repeated with eerie mimicry, causing great offence. She saw another danger: she began to teach him new lyrics to Ian Dury: *ducks & geese & fox & mole*, they sang along in the car.

About this time the TV text on the screen began to bother her. It flashed huge white letters against a blue screen: *Sell Your Car!* The car horn blared mysteriously in the middle of the night. The driver's door was found to be open. She went down and closed it.

Someone made an appointment for her at the GP's; the same one who looked after her recent throat infection and knew she worked at the theatre. It should have been all right, but she confused 11am with 1pm by writing the numerals too close together. So when she arrived at the surgery at one o'clock there was a pincer movement towards her to remove the child, who hadn't had his hair washed in weeks. Neglect of the child reported by the schoolteachers was allied to reports from her new neighbours that she was planting paper in pots of soil.

But the pain didn't start until the social workers set her up with a therapist. It started after the first session. When she pressed her foot to the floor of the car she got electric shocks into her spine. She had to give up driving. She began to walk to the school to pick up the boy.

The pain continued. She would suddenly cry out from the shock when she pressed the keys of her computer. So she stopped using it.

After the initial assessment, where she admitted her husband had left and she was worried about money, she agreed to see another counsellor. He had two rooms. The outer room was blue and the inner room was green. When it rained, the blue room was always a shade darker to wait in. And she was relieved to get into the green room where he kept an amber lamp lit on his desk.

What's it like out?

It's raining, she says.

You're Irish.

I am.

I'm Welsh.

You don't have an accent.

I had it beaten out of me, he said. Where would you like to sit?

He indicates a choice of easy chairs, which she rejects. She takes a hard chair from the wall and places it next to the armchair facing his.

So who is sitting in that chair?

Well, I don't think I'm Goldilocks. I have Spain in my pine.

Say again.

Pain in my spine.

What has triggered it?

I'm at the end of my tether. And by the way I can't pay for this, beyond this session.

You're not paying for this, you were referred. You were about to be sectioned.

Why?

Why did you try to plant paper in the flowerpots?

I buried paper in the flowerpots to hide what I'd written down. I was afraid. Am I not allowed to feel afraid?

Are you not allowed to feel afraid? He says.

She knows she cannot tell him anything that won't result in seeming paranoid. And she recognises the great risk she runs of the child being taken into care; the unfairness of it. She didn't know why she didn't mention it, to anyone, that day in the Botanic Gardens when the band was playing in the Edwardian white ironwork filigree bandstand, and the peacocks trailing green and blue iridescence screamed on the grass.

They think we're a Trojan Horse, she says.

And for the first time she felt she'd hit her mark. There is a flicker in his eyes.

Imagine that, a single woman and a little boy. And every time he leaves my sight I think he's going to disappear.

Why?

Father sat at the table in his vest and trousers. He had never done this at my grandmother's house when I was growing up. I felt it acutely as an affront to my shy adolescence. In fact, it was a rebuke to my mother's aspirations. She wanted deliverance. He was showing her – you married me.

The arguments between us grew. I find words to reject his form of politics in which style dominated substance.

You think you're a working-class hero sitting at the table in a vest to eat your dinner.

Look in the mirror, he shouted back! No old man down the country would trust a woman in a floppy hat and a long flowering skirt coming to tell him he needs a job and a vote.

It was the start of my standing up to him. By the end of the summer I would return to find my mother clinging to the banisters crying 'get me out of here someone please.'

It was the events of those four days in January 1969 that were to change the dynamic between us.

The first day of the march was the first day of the year, and I got the bus to the city centre. They were half-way up Donegall Place when I caught up with them.

The bus was packed with people going to work. I got on with my rucksack. There was a curious silence which I couldn't understand. I was looking at my own reflection in the glass of the driver's seat three rows back. I was properly dressed for once. Cords, a green weatherproof coat with a hood, and black boots.

I was still at school so free to do something the people on the bus could not do. I wasn't risking a job; I didn't have any money, and school didn't start until after the Feast of the Epiphany. Their concentration made me aware of the moment I was in, which is why I remember it so clearly. They saw me even with their eyes closed, some of them on the early shift; they saw me when I didn't see myself. The hushed silence of the bus alerted me.

The marchers were a small group, no more than thirty, and none of the leaders were there at that time of the morning as I recall.

Father wasn't around for the first couple of days, I'm sure. But he turned up about the third day offering his car and he took some of the luggage. I pretended not to know him. He was a worker, he looked like a worker. I was posing as a student. I pretended he wasn't my father. It was all down to the Persian Prince and my mother's theatrical ambitions. I was skilled at passing.

The man in the green room wants to know who the Persian Prince is. I explain it's a drawing of a costume for a character in Shakespeare.

I need to tell you about the morning of the attack. It was the fourth day of January.

I can feel his patience wearing thin; I delivered long monologues in those days.

It was tense because we still had the final arrival into Derry, and we have been blamed in the press for riots in several towns along the way. Maghera, the nearest county town, for instance, an Orange Hall had been burned. Several older members of the civil rights executive blamed us for worsening sectarian tensions.

By this stage on the final morning there were hundreds lined up. Every time we attracted opposition more people joined. Our ranks were swollen and quite a few from the mid-Ulster villages, most of whom were not students, joined. We were at the front because it was our group who walked from the City Hall. It began to look like a medieval army moving among high hedges towards a little bridge.

Then there was a shout. A man wearing denim ran down the hilly field above us, followed by a pile of stones, and glass jars that were full of small black grit and exploded on impact with the surface of the road. I thought they looked like the empty coffee jars we used to drink out of in the balmy summer of '67 in a flat on the Beersbridge Road.

And to avoid the missiles that had begun to rain down onto the road, where a big space had opened up from the people in front of me, we ran down through the fields towards the river. And into the river, and we braced it. There were men on both banks with cudgels and sticks, and then they came into the river. Sarah was a swimmer so she wouldn't drown, I thought. But it was freezing. We were accompanied by another young female marcher who I didn't know. In fact we had followed her to the river. Then one of our friends, a big guy I had never spoken to, appeared behind the lads with cudgels who were approaching us. The river was fast-flowing and one of the attackers was very close.

Hey, come on lads, what are you going to do? Three wee girls and you with cudgels would fell a bull.

We all stood waiting, knee deep in water. I became afraid of losing my footing. I believe if anyone had fallen it would have started.

Come on lads, what are you going to do?

He was a big fellow. Red-haired. Milk-fed skin. No one spoke.

Then inexplicably the lads with cudgels turned away, climbed the banks and went after youths on the road.

You were lucky, the man in the green room said. And your time is up.

We were lucky because our rescuer turned out to be Maria's brother; she was the girl who went into the river with us. He had forbidden her to go on the march because he said it was too dangerous. Later, she told me she had been working at a petrol pump on the Maghera Road, when my father came by with a car full of sleeping bags. She said she'd love to go on the march with the students, so he went back and got her when she finished work, and he drove her into the village to join the rest of us. So I reckon he was responsible for her being in the river with me. I was glad nothing bad happened to us.

The man in the green room was on his feet, and he switched off the amber lamp.

One of the parents, a school governor, invited me to her house, while Dan was being taken care of by another parent. We are sitting opposite a catholic church. I hadn't noticed this before; I could see it through the bay windows of the room we were in. I knew it was a catholic church because it said in big letters on the front *Catholic Church*.

I'd been brought up to hide my religion, so I thought *wow, that is confident.*

How do you get into the theatre, she asked? My son would like to be an actor. What would he have to do?

I don't know. I started when I was a child, it was my mother's ambition originally.

She doesn't like my answer because she says: what makes one want to show off?

I started to tell the school governor that it has something to do with the fact that on a wet cold November Sunday afternoon you go into the theatre and people are hammering up a set and turning the hall into a woodland with fauns and running streams and bird sounds in the trees. Or she'd suddenly find herself in the inner courtyard of the Grand Vizier's Palace, trailing bougainvillea petals on the surface of a pool. And it was sunlight when the operator of the follow spot turned the lamps on you, while outside on the street it was grey with rain.

The social workers can't get in there, the woman interrupts.

In where?

To the theatre. Actors keep very much to themselves. How do you get to be an actor? Who chooses? Who says what face goes on tv? Who says who gets in? She mentions a famous name and adds: I grew up with them. They used to come to our children's parties. They drove around in a bus.

The actor she mentions is famous for making an aristocratic marriage; I wonder if this is at the heart of the governor's concern. Is the theatre possibly a back door, a fast track into society? A society whose exits and entrances are so closely monitored. In the end the governor is asking: how did you get in here? How did you get so close to us? What lies are you performing that we took you for one of us? The woman looks at her calmly for a long time. They haven't been talking about the theatre at all; they have been talking about the school.

New neighbours have moved into the cul-de-sac. They are standing, mother and son, on the patio in the evening light looking across an enclosed field to the houses on the other side. There's a sunset, it's vivid and everything has a pinkish glow. She is thinking that soon probably this field will also fill up with houses. And for the moment they are lucky. Then music fills the empty playing fields and she says: oh listen.

No. They use the beautiful music. It's a trap. And he goes inside and slides the door shut. He watches her bewilderment.

She stands on the stone paving and tries to open the door, but he will not let her. When he lets go of the door, she slides it open. And for the second time she finds herself asking: who are they?

He shakes his head. I feel so betrayed.

Do you know what that word means? She asks.

No, I don't. But Ali says it all the time.

Then why do you say it?

It's how I feel. It sounds so sad.

And why are you sad?

Because you are so ill.

She is astonished. Is that how I appear to you? And then she says: would you like to throw the ball to me? We have our short-handled tennis rackets in the garage. We could play a tennis game in front of the house.

On the road? He asks hopefully.

She nods: there is no one around. She means the new neighbour who doesn't seem to like children. He has sent his own away to boarding school, and rings the police if he sees any in the cul-de-sac.

He agrees, but after a while he finds she can't keep score. She taught him to score tennis; Love 15. Love 30. 15–30.

But something has happened to her mind. Try to keep score, he says.

You mustn't worry about me anymore, she says.

He laughs at her. Then he says: this makes it all worthwhile. All the stings. I can put up with it now.

The word stings plays back and forth in her mind in the quietly-echoing close.

Deuce.

They continue to pass the ball between them until the light goes. But she can't keep track of the score. All she can do is return the ball.

Once they realised I didn't know the secret they thought I was so skilfully evading, they lost interest in me.

She is still managing to get acting work during this period. She makes an appearance on *Crimetime* because her agent knows she needs the cash. And she happens to find herself in a break with another actor, Samir Khan. He is holding out a coffee to her when he says: 'Asians don't like luvvies.'

Are you Hindu or Muslim, Samir? I never know the difference.

Are you Catholic or Protestant? You all look the same to me, he says.

I grew up in the north of Ireland. I lived in Scandinavia. The Vikings I know about! What experience do I have of Asians?

My name is Khan. That's a big clue.

Like Ghengis.

Not like Ghengis.

Why do Asians not like luvvies?

They think it's telling lies. Then he asks, will you go for a drink afterwards?

I have the kid with me because they've suspended him from school for a week. And I've no one to look after him today.

What did he do?

He's a mimic. He repeats things off the TV from programmes he's not supposed to be watching!

He might be an actor.

I don't want him to be an actor.

How did you ever get into acting?

My mother was a dressmaker. One day she walked up to our drama teacher and said: she dances along the top of the sideboard and sings to herself in the mirror. If you give her a part in plays I'll make the costumes. And Peggy Piper knew a good deal when she saw it. The demand was so great Mother went into partnership with Auntie Maud, and moved from a Singer sewing machine to electric.

Mine owned a souk in Leicester, Lamps and Turkish carpets, beeswax soap and silk bedspreads. She found me one day draped in a bolt of her raw silk; I had added kohl to my eyes. I was dancing in front of my cousins. She packed me off to business college but I found the drama class. I really wanted to be a dancer.

I only ever wanted to be a writer.

I heard you're on the screenplay of *Arabian Nights*.

I'm only writing one of the tales, and even then I'm part of a team.

My brother-in-law has a flat in Malta. Are they filming there?

I'm not allowed to say any more.

Sure.

There's a buzz from the location manager's headset and a signal to say they are ready for us, when Samir says, with a big smile, as we walk towards the location: I was in an episode of *Crimetime* a few months ago, and someone, another Asian, rang up and reported my name to the police. I was arrested. I had to explain that I was an actor, and the televised scene was an enactment of the burglary, and that they ought to speak to the police on the programme.

And did they?

Yeah, but only after I spent several hours in a cell, but I also learnt that the person who rang the police was an uncle of mine. A little bit of me thinks that both the uncle and the police who arrested me knew all along I was an actor.

I tell him about the school governor. And add, Asians aren't the only ones who don't like luvvies.

Have you told him his father has left?

No.

Tell him, Samir says.

In that summer, in the last days of June, there were thunder storms. Once again she had the feeling prompted by the weather that there were forces bringing their world to an end, and that there were only so many places left on the transport to the new planet, and to be allowed to enter they were all being judged on how they behaved now. She was really very ill.

At the same time she could see graffiti on the new red-brick wall at the entrance to the cul-de-sac. Some slogan relating to White Wolves and Vinland was painted on the wall. The images reminded her of Sweden, but she didn't think it had anything to do with her. And then it was painted over and replaced with the words, *Wet Wet Wet.*

The cement mixer was silent. The houses were complete. They named the street in which she now lived. Also out of the blue the post arrived directly: Julius had invited her to come to Ireland with the child. He lived, with various generations of his family, on one of those peninsulas where the first incursions began, he explained. She had to make a narrative to convince the man with the lamp that she was worthy of sanity and capable of it and could be released to take care of the child and the car.

There are no Persian Princes in Shakespeare, my mother insisted when presented with the drawing of my costume.

It's from A Midsummer Night's Dream, *I insist. I quote Oberon and Titania's exchange about my character.*

I do but beg a little changeling boy to be my henchman.

His mother was a votaress of my order ... And for her sake I will not part with him.

But you don't have any lines! My mother protested.

No, even more reason that I look impressive.

How am I supposed to make a turban?

It's a band of cloth which you pin.

What kind of feather is that?

It's from a peacock.

Where am I going to find a peacock feather? she complains.

I go off to the kitchen cabinet and bring her a bottle of Camp Coffee. It is one of those items that we had in the house, but nobody worked out how to drink. There's a man in a turban on the label and he's serving coffee to a woman languishing on a cushion. I think we bought it for the picture.

He's hardly a prince, my mother observed.

No. But he's Persian, I lied stoutly.

But I know she will make it when she consults Peggy Piper's drawing again: there are two feathers, cut close to the eye, and pinned with a brooch. And I know that she will also consult Auntie Maud, who's in business with her.

It's only a fecking turban, Auntie Maud said when mother showed her the drawing. Look at this, I've got to make a fecking cobweb. She held up a limp piece of chainmail.

What is that? my mother asked.

Fishing net and purple spray to finish. That woman has my head turned.

It looks like an old string vest.

I am standing on the table with my back to the door, and my head is swathed in slippery but light cut-up parachute silk, god knows from where. There's a large pin from my kilt holding everything together on my head. Auntie Maud has taken over the task from my mother who prefers making dresses. She has just pinned a panel of lilac silk onto a tunic of flowering chintz, somebody's chair cover. She is looking at a picture: Persian (Safavid) seated artist late 16th century. The book is open on the stool beneath the window. We can't figure out because the scribes are seated what they are wearing on their legs, but she had made me a pair of pale blue pantaloons. Because it is hot in the room, my head is beginning to sweat. I know better than to complain or to move a muscle. I have always been her favourite to dress because I'm good at staying still.

Suddenly she says: what are you thinking?

I was about to answer her when a voice says: I came to you first.

You should walk on down to the printers. They can get you away tonight.

I'm not going away.

This is the first place they will look for you.

I've been released. They won't be coming for me. We've all been released.

Auntie Maud placed her pinking shears very carefully down on the table. Her scissors cut the material, leaving an edge of little triangles.

My husband? My brother? When?

I haven't a baldy. One hour. Two.

That's enough for now, she said, helping me off the table.

It was then that I turned and saw the old man, for the first time, waiting in the corner.

She lifted the book and handed it to me. On the front of the library book the title said: Gentile Bellini's Persian Album.

You go home to your mother, and take this with you. Tell her to finish it.

She unwound the turban from my head as if removing a bandage.

So what kind of week have you had? the man with the lamp asked.

She tries to remember the days.

What about the neighbourhood, do you still feel afraid?

A number of children from the surrounding estate came into the cul-de-sac to play with my boy. And the neighbours complained. They didn't like the strange children. They said the kids mimicked them and stole their flower pots. We had to send them away. In our old neighbourhood everybody mixed.

Why did you move?

When my husband left, the house was too big for me, and I couldn't pay the mortgage. She went on, my son was brought up next to a family of Asian girls. When the cousins arrived they put him back over the fence.

Doesn't your son have other friends?

Yes. At school.

She won't name any friends because she has got it into her head that someone will harm them.

Ali's mother made her sit in the garden in the sun. She brought food. Stuffed dates, warm apples packed with rice and pine nuts.

In the old neighbourhood the women dried their carpets on her fence, which she didn't like, but they brought her naan the size of a duvet and balti chicken which she did like. She remembers the women arriving with a tray of food handcooked in their own dishes when she was in the grip of a *Godfather* script and felt annoyed at being interrupted in her work. She feels ashamed at her own insouciance about their gift.

She describes an elaborate feast in the glow of the lamp because the reality is evading her. She wonders how many years of pain she'd have saved herself and the boy if she'd repeated what the old man had said: but the word, like a fish, slipped from her grasp. Mercenaries. She does not remember in time. Nor the moment when that long bow drew back.

Can you have his eyes tested, he seems a bit short-sighted, the young English teacher said in passing on her way to the car. The teacher slammed the door shut. Why is everybody so cross with me, she thought.

After the eye test she goes with him to collect the wired-framed glasses; they were in three colours, red and blue and green. Which she hopes will appease him for having to wear them. He steps into the street beside her, and falls back: wow!

She turns to look at him. What is it?

I can see the writing across the name of the road. I can see the numbers on the houses. The colours are very bright, he says.

She had not been seeing the boy; had been blind to what everyone was trying to tell her. Even as she approached their escape to Julius, she was considering leaving him there so that she could return to work. She wasn't even holding him in her mind, because her mind was in full flight.

And if the birds that had unearthed the pieces of her shattered mind had flown down instead and reassembled the pages, they might have preserved for her an image for later years, of a mind unable to bear the knowledge of what had happened to it.

I lean over backwards and view the room upside down – a glass wall separates the dance studio from the swimming pool below, so that when I look at the world I see the vast empty space of the ceiling above the pool, the air in the rectangle spreading like mercury behind the glass partition, making a mirror for me. I am looking at my own mind and it has emptied. The air is full of other people's lines.

A few weeks later she hears the word Srebrenica for the first time. It is the 11th of July, 1995. She remembers: young men working on building sites lured to Bosnia with a promise. Was there a kill fee for each Muslim man they took off the bus?

If she had passed on the old man's message about the mercenaries, perhaps the massacre wouldn't have taken place.

The man with the amber lamp is dismissive. He wants to know what story she was trying to burn. What had she written that the birds had exhumed?

Exhumed? He actually uses the word exhumed.

I told you about the attack on the student march.

There are things we cannot bear to know about ourselves, he said.

Perhaps what you need is a witness. It's the last thing he says to me, that summer. Perhaps if you can't hold anything in your mind, or your body, then you need to find somewhere else to put these experiences, until you are well enough to –

I'm a writer, she interrupts him.

I opened some cream vellum parchment and wrote in the journal in pencil. I was afraid to commit my words to a screen; I had felt someone else was reading them. I couldn't even risk writing in ink.

I saw Maud a few years later, after the night I saw the old man in the corner of her room for the first time, and she sent me packing with my turban. She had stopped making costumes since that time; though my mother continued alone with the business.

I was standing in the middle of the Falls; a hundred and one days since the start of the year 1969. I was addressing a large crowd and telling them to walk with me to the police station to hand in a petition. Maud stood grimly in front of me.

Stop this now, I understand your anger, but you have no authority here.

You misunderstand. I'm not angry. I'm trying to get them to —

To follow you to the police station! Are you really that stupid?

The fear is making an orphan of my thoughts.

A young couple moved next door; they were more tolerant of the presence of children. She discovered they were Sikh when the man rang the doorbell to deliver a redirected letter. He wore a turban. The letter was from Julius and contained a map.

Twenty-five years on along that road, his mother sat down on the same sofa in the place where the lamp shone. It was not the same house. It was where she placed him as a baby when she had to work, watching him from her seat at the desk, where he now sat reading her journal. The summer of 1995.

Are we over it? she asks, when he looks up from reading.

Is it true? he asks.

At the same time he noticed that some pages were missing from the front of the journal.

When I return from the interrupted costume-fitting my father is getting ready to go on night shift.

Maud says you're to finish it.

Aye, the internees have been released, my father says. She'll be busy.

How did that happen? Mother asks.

The Trades Council guaranteed the IRA would not return to a sectarian campaign.

And the government believed them?

The Protestant workers on the Trades Council are very influential.

You mean the Communists.

All of us. Catholics and Protestants.

Times have changed.

Is m'daddy a Communist then? she asks after her father has gone to work.

Don't be daft. If you only spoke to the people you agree with in this town you'd be very lonely.

I saw Auntie Maud a few years later; she had stopped making costumes, while mother continued. She was standing in the middle of the Falls Road, a hundred and one days since the start of the year 1969. I was addressing a large crowd and telling them to walk with me to the police station to hand in a petition. Maud stood grimly in front of me.

Stop this now. I understand your anger but you have no authority here.

You misunderstand. I'm not angry. I'm trying to get them to —

To follow you to the police station, she intervened. Are you really that stupid?

She was backed by a line of older girls and women, and for the first time I realised who she was and what she was in command of. She didn't need their mocking chorus. I stopped right there on the road. Power always wants to reveal itself.

Fear is making an orphan of her past.

You were with those students.

The woman approached her at a literary festival in the park where she had given a reading. Dan was with her, and they were feeding the ducks.

Yes, she says. I was with those students.

The face had not been friendly. And the question rhetorical. Her fear of Dan disappearing from her sight had become unboundaried again. Her senses were amplified. Her alertness supercharged. Nothing happened.

A few days after that she was alone making her way to the carpark through the shopping mall. She was about to turn off towards the tunnel of concrete which would take her to the lift shaft – she had parked her car on the fifth floor of the multi-storey – when she became aware that someone had looked at her with malign intent. There were hundreds of people around her. They were walking in every direction. But no one was going into the long service corridor. She walked quickly towards the rubber doors which separated the tunnel from the entrance to the lifts. She remembered they were slow; one of them was out of order. So she would be standing in the well of the concrete staircase until the lift reached her. She had no proof she would be followed into the tunnel, but she was convinced that her mind had touched the mind of something ominous. At the moment when she reached the end of the tunnel the doors from the shopping mall opened behind her. She turned to look back, and a giant of a man some six foot and seventeen stone of weight entered the corridor. He was wearing a puffer jacket. His body was so wide it filled the whole passage width. There was only herself at one end and him at the other. If she went on she would be trapped by the steel doors of the lift shalt. So she turned, and instead of running away from him, she ran towards him with all her might roaring, a war cry such as Boudicea would not have been ashamed of, or some warrior amazon. The giant was wide-eyed when she rushed up to him. She ran on past, taking his surprise as a trophy. Two men in fluorescent yellow jackets were mounting a new street name to the red-brick wall at the entrance to the enclave when she returned. Dallas Plaza was what it said.

What happened to your glasses? she asked, as they drove away from the enclave with their map.

I don't need them. They're for school.

They aren't just for school.

I miss the blur.

What blur?

The blur at the centre of things, he said.

A Place called Dam

One morning in Amsterdam she woke from a dream about the sea. She was floating on her back, a great wave suspended above her. Everything was still; she existed in the seconds before the wave collapsed on top of her. And that was the day he left her.

She got off the tram first, while he remained, fumbling by the doors which shut behind her; when she turned he had been carried away with a clang by the tram. She started to walk on, to follow the direction of the tram lines, but it proved too fast. It swerved around a corner away in the distance and disappeared. He had organised this excursion to a more industrial part of the city, but now she was lost. She hadn't been paying attention because she was relying on him. It was then she looked down and saw on the cobbled pavement a pair of old boots. The uncanniness arrested her. She had earlier stood in front of Van Gogh's painting of two left boots in the museum. The boots on the street resembled Van Gogh's, except for an upturned empty bottle in one of them. She took a photograph on the new phone: it masked that other image, blocked it from her memory, of his face behind the shut glass doors of the tram, expressionless, as they separated.

She collected herself, then she called him. Her phone showed 'Call Ended'. She tried again, his name lit up, but the call ended. She kept trying again and again. And then she stopped and walked back to a big junction where many tram lines met. A place called Dam. A neo-classical building dominated the site; it was a palace of some kind. She found herself, seated at the tram stop, looking up underneath a towering figure holding a sphere on his shoulders. Hercules? As if he was about to drop the world on her. It reminded her of that dream of waiting under the wave. She felt it tremble above her all day.

Two men noticed her, because it is a busy stop with people coming and going, but she has remained sitting for a long time. She thinks of ringing her son. What would she say: I'm worried he's wandered off and isn't answering his phone? She knows it's wrong to call him. But her finger touches the ring sign and she finds she has called him; she ends the call immediately. And when she does, her partner rings up and gets through.

I'm at Central Railway Station, he says. I need to top up my tram card.

I'm at a place called Dam, we passed through it.

Go on back to the hotel on the next tram, he says.

I'll wait for you, she insists.

The night they arrived, she remembers emerging from the railway station to a barricade of bicycles. If I'd come here on my own I might have ridden one, she thought. She could ride one now, but he might struggle.

She was writing a film script about Van Gogh. He wanted to come to Amsterdam with her. But now she saw he was changing his mind. She saw it in his hesitancy when finally he got off the tram. I bet he turns away in the opposite direction, she thinks, and he does. She doesn't go after him. She will wait at the stop until he returns. The light is going to blink, it's her favourite time, or it should have been. Here they are together and yet he looks drawn and seems to have difficulty walking.

Perhaps he's like Van Gogh, she thinks. We have taken him for a mad man, but really, he is a saint. She has spent the first day in the Van Gogh Museum in front of *The Potato Eaters*. The painting shocked her.

She told him about it at lunchtime. It's a family eating in a room, but it is under a miner's lamp. They were fouled by dirt, none of the dignity of the outdoor peasants of Corot or Pissarro attaches to them, only this grimy gloom in the yellow flame of the lamp. Because one of them was underground digging out their existence, they were all down there.

The picture had gathered her into its atmosphere since she'd seen it. It was her own roots she was looking at; her father's family coming in from the country to the dirty old town for work. Her grandmother. What did they call the Irish in England in the '80s? The potato eaters. She was a handsome woman, her father's mother, with enough confidence to commission an oval photograph of the three of them: her eyes widened in hope, holding up her first born, next to her diffident husband. 1925. And he still deaf from the First World War trench bombardment.

It hung in the hall of the family house in Belfast. Of course they couldn't maintain the glossy optimism of that commissioned photograph; they worked in dust, from the flax mills, the timber yards, the coal yards. It was her generation who got the nice work that allowed them to sustain the glossy life. But even they had begun to descend a decade ago when the credit tide receded; it was always only on loan, that access to a life above ground.

In the afternoon when, alone again, she found herself in front of Rembrandt's *The Jewish Bride*, she began to cry. She felt she was looking at her husband. Yet, he filled her with irritation when she was standing in front of him. She could only cry for him in front of the painting. Perhaps it was the bride's red dress? She knew Van Gogh stood before this painting for many hours. *The Potato Eaters* made her feel guilty.

Suddenly, at the tram interchange, he is plunging past her.

This isn't our stop.

She knows that he has tried to take her to the industrial part of the city because he wants to confront her with their real existence, whereas this trip has been a respite. She had got them rooms in the old city, in a leafy thoroughfare of old Dutch houses, with a balcony onto the park; a glockenspiel punctuating the day, reminding her of her youthful beginnings in Germany in the '70s; her own eyes widened in hope at the memory. It infuriated him. She tries to reason about the tram stop. They have been conversing loudly in a foreign city as if no one can understand them, but in fact everyone around speaks English.

An American intervenes; this is your tram stop.

Thank you for your help, he says, but we don't need it.

He walks off again. This time she follows him. They must be careful crossing the tram lines in the wide cobbled square because the bicycles are so silent and seem to come from four different directions at once. Also, the islands to stand in between different parts of the road, tram tracks, bicycle lanes, pedestrian pavements, are so narrow and closely graphed and charted, she has never been anywhere with so many boundaries in such proximity. They have gone a long way to find the further stop when an Asian guy points out these trams are all going to the Amsterdam Centraal railway station.

We need to go in the opposite direction, she says. We need to go back to the stop where you got off at Dam.

She walks on back on her own, carefully crossing the lines, occasionally glancing to see if he is following. When she reaches the intersection at Dam she sits down again; three trams to their neighbourhood pass but she is still waiting, and he finally arrives when the fourth tram is about to depart. He gets on at one end and she at the other. They meet again when they get back to the square in their neighbourhood.

It is 10pm. It was seven thirty when they set out.

Where would you like to eat? He asks, as if nothing has happened.

They go to the nearby terrace of the American Hotel where she drinks a glass of red wine and feels defeated. The moment at Dam is not fleeting; it is permanent, she realises. I have sat there all my life.

The woman's tongue slipped out like a lizard catching a fly, and discreetly withdrew again. It was this mannerism that she vaguely recalled from somewhere years ago which triggered the impulse to take a photo.

From the moment they arrived in the city she felt herself hurtling. She was fast, but time seemed to slow down, and everyone's actions seemed to be slower, at variance with time itself. Halfway down one of the long thoroughfares that mimic the canal ring south they find a restaurant. The head waiter beckons them towards a table on the outside patio just at the window with a good view of the passing street. It is a glass-partitioned space between two nightclubs. They are at the back of the patio with two tables in front of them. Her companion tries to hurry the proceedings: excuse me, excuse me, before she can restrain him. The waiter squares up to him: this is the time of evening, he says, when I like to take it easy.

He places the menus down with some water and glasses. It is the waiter who touches her shoulder in reassurance, firmly in control of the evening's entertainment. Four men in white t-shirts with D-cups and blonde wigs and red lipstick, not so much trannies as pantomime dames, stop in the middle of the street to have their photo taken. They are joined by another wearing a blonde wig on his head and a black wig dangling between his legs. Another photo is taken, before they all move off.

The Italians keep up friendly banter with the bouncers next door offering tinfoil batons of garlic bread, while the doormen at the bottom of the next-door staircase keep revellers moving into the random procession along the street. A group of young people in shorts and jeans, some wearing similar pink and purple t-shirts, are the next group along and seem to belong to a small herd. The t-shirts have the same words: *you have been amsterdamed.* It's not a continuous movement; spaces open and reveal walkers strolling after dinner, or families of tourists making their way back, trying to keep their children from looking around too much. Another group carry away a bay tree from the restaurant terrace and are chased by the waiter. They're young, he says indulgently, and plants it down at the entrance. It had been dropped some way along the street.

She has finished a glass of red wine and eaten half the pizza when it dawns on her: we're the oldest people here. The table in front is full of young Asian women and men; the men are looking at their phones while the women are eating seafood pasta. A middle-aged woman arriving alone gets a table near them. This waiter has been kind to us, she thinks, giving us a ringside table. I could have come here on my own after all, she thinks. The light looks about to go. Suddenly, with the coming notes of a skin drum struck, it is gone and night falls like a curtain. That's when the lantern carriers appear.

The first part of the procession of revellers are women carrying branches of almond blossom, cherry and apple. Some of the blooms fall onto the tables and at their feet. Some of the women are wearing medieval costumes and accompanied by minstrels with lutes and other stringed instruments. They are followed by a noisy group impossible to match in its rowdiness and colour, most of whom are carrying brooms and look like mermaids or sea witches with dark rust tendrils of glistening waist length hair. They are accompanied by men on bikes in caps and bells; identifiably they are the fools. The final section puzzles her. The women wear long gowns and veils in blue and white and some of them carry blackthorn sticks with huge musky roses attached. But they look as if they have walked through the desert.

What am I looking at? She asks her companion.

The Australian woman at the next table says it is the opening of the music and theatre festival.

But what does it mean? Why are they carrying almond blossom?

The first group are love's warriors; women who know how to love. Then come the promiscuous ones, who say yes to everyone. Hence the noise. Finally the last group are the virgins who remain chaste. They are rewarded with this dust. Have a leaflet. The woman hands over a flyer. You should come and see us in the park tomorrow among the sculptures. There's an Irish play in the festival. You're Irish, aren't you?

We're from Belfast.

Yes, I like the way you speak English, she says. There used to be lots of Irish here, years ago. Now there are not so many.

You have an Australian accent yourself.

Only when I speak English, the woman says. I'm married to an Australian. I'm a native of this city.

Maybe we should go, her companion says, observing a pause in the procession.

We can't. He's not going to give us our bill and there's more to come.

She has a long view of the street and can see a group of dancers arrive in golden shifts with gold makeup. They appear to be dancing statues. Some are carrying conch shells.

These are Indonesian temple dancers, the woman says. They represent sacred prostitutes of both genders.

Are they performers or sex workers? He asks.

They are performers. I imagine the sex workers would prefer this parade to standing in tacky windows in the Red Light District.

At that moment two young females approach the table and kiss the woman on either side of her face. One is taller than the other. They are Chinese. They sit down beside her and begin to speak Dutch, until she breaks off to address a waiter. Can you bring my daughters a menu?

Another waiter places their bill on the table, she examines it and pays in euro. Her companion makes a move.

Don't leave yet, the woman says, it's nearly over, but you must wait for the hares to pass. The woman smiles when she says this: it's good fun.

At that moment hares walking on hind legs and carrying bows and arrows appear in the street. Then come the women and men in black with white skeletons painted on the cloth, luminous like ghost train paint. They too are dancers. She lifts her phone to take a photo of the giant hare in the middle of the parade, when a thin female face with a silver cap of hair turned to look at her as she takes the photo. It was then the tongue came out, tracing the bottom lip as if sealing an envelope. She could hear distant pipes. Let's go before the flute band gets here, she says.

She stood in the middle of the lake on the ice that would not exist when she returned. Circumstances would combine to change so dramatically that the environment that sustained her, and people like her, would disappear. She was simply one of a species is what her companion told her.

The lake was still frozen in front of the student settlement when they set off. A good sign, Johann said. It meant there would still be snow further west on the slopes in Austria. They could take their skis. She marvelled at his unrelenting enthusiasm. The drive was along the northern shores of the Bodensee. Early April sunlight glinted on the slopes of the presiding mountains, commanding awe. Sometimes they would pass through a hamlet where plump bolsters flung from an upper open shutter. They don't agree about the music on the radio, except that they both like jazz which is hard to find. He likes Wagner, she hates Georgian chant; a piece of Borodin unites them, she remembers it as Stranger in Paradise. *Mostly they drove in silence, until in the late afternoon they are still close to the Bodensee when a deep base voice on the radio finds them.*

There's an old man called the Mississippi
That's the old man that I''d like to be
What does he care if the world's got troubles
What does he care if the land ain't free ...

Her father sang it. Robeson was his great hero. The deep weariness of the world she is fleeing overtakes her. They drove on in snow chains on the passes that remained open.

They stopped in the Tyrol for the night in a cool room that the housewife had advertised with a sign in the window. They offer to pay in deutschemarks which the housewife is happy with, she would wait to get Austrian schillings in Salzburg. Even so, when she looked, she already had four currencies in her purse.

They slept on twin beds pushed together under bolsters that sat like tumulus clouds on the mattress; at first she feels smothered and then cold beneath the volume of bedding, until he says come here. They share a whiskey kiss and the warmth spreads.

She wakes from a dream in which lake ice is melting; she must stay ahead of the rapid thaw. She tells him at breakfast: I dreamt I skied across a lake and the ice turned to water behind me. I made it just in time, and I was exhausted and lay down.

It's hardly surprising you dreamt that, you've just described the ride across Lake Constance, Johann says. The Bodensee is Lake Constance. We drove along it all day yesterday. The story goes a man is riding all night in a snow storm until finally he arrives at a village; they ask him from what direction he came, and he points it out to them. You've just ridden across Lake Constance, on the ice, the villagers tell him. At the knowledge he drops dead from fright. The moral, don't look back. It's the looking back that kills the traveller.

His sentiment opens a chasm between them that he is unaware off, and she has not found a way to challenge. Before the details of her journey vanished she would commit them to paper.

Memories are what age us, she writes in her notebook in Amsterdam on the balcony overlooking the park. The new camera allows her to make notes; it is like a prosthetic limb, a hearing aid or a telescope. She can make visual notes during the day and then recollect them later to find she's made a sequence. From the balcony onto the park on the first day she had taken a photo of a tree. It caught her attention because on one side the leaves were already dead, while the other side was thriving. Supposing she was looking at a brain, her brain, one side of which was ageing prematurely like the tree. The new camera brought the dead side to life. She had cognitive function but not episodic. The camera would help her hide the disability. But the camera had also the ability to capture movement; it seemed to be a combination of film and still. She has taken a photo of him sitting on the balcony looking at a white bird which moves off the wall before the image comes to a halt. And each time she reviews the pose, the bird lifts off the wall. Equally in the photo she has taken of the hares and the dancers, the woman's lick appears again and again.

The next day they go out on a barge on the canal and experience a sense of calm at being on water. Because she has spent the morning with him she can return to the galleries in the afternoon. He doesn't want to walk anywhere.

After she has left *The Jewish Bride*, she walks through the hall of honour in the Rijksmuseum until she finds herself among the audience for a moment in a play: it is the moment of movement before everyone settles into place. There is an entire school party seated on the gallery floor drawing characters from it. Rembrandt has called this scene, *The Night Watch*. It's the second time this week she has looked at it. Its gravitational pull has stopped her from going into the chamber behind the painting, which she proceeds to do, up a short flight of steps and into a room of sculptures. She finds herself at Dam Square again, only this time it is as if she has flown to the top of the palace roof.

The sculptures in the room are from various parts of the city, brought inside to preserve them. The stone women, originally placed on either side of Hercules, are described as Wisdom and Justice. The missing limbs suggested they are not fakes. At any rate, they are not what confounds her. Instead it is a female Lacoon figure which seems to be struggling with a python. It dominates the middle of the room. She doesn't want to look at it. When she goes to read the note on the wall, she finds that she is mistaken about the python. She is looking at a sandstone statue called *Frenzy*. A woman is tearing out her hair while standing on a plinth, and a madman is looking out from under the sides of the plinth on which she is standing. The date is 1660. It has been retrieved from the grounds of the madhouse. The woman's face is contorted with pain and her tongue is lolling in her mouth. The sculpture is by Artus Quellinus. She learns then that madhouse in Dutch is *dolhuys*.

In my statue haunted childhood, she thinks, the Virgin Mary, Saint Teresa of Avila, the Pieta, the complexes of my grandmother's mind, came to me as part of an inheritance; the hard wiring of childhood saints. Once in Rome she had taken photos of various female stone saints which, compared with the composure of classical women, looked like demonstrations of hysteria. Her shock at the discovery of the madwoman is mitigated when she finds a Vermeer, *Woman Reading a Letter*, her cool blue smock against a yellow wall. She stops and opens her notebook: 'yellow casts a cool blue shadow' she writes, echoing the guide notes. All the time she is looking for the one strengthening image, a kind of unity. Who am I now?

I don't know, she thinks, if it is a matter of costume changes, or if it's character, or if there is no such thing, no such self, no unity but the place and situation which creates a self, like a wave rising and dissolving into the next place. In different places and different situations she felt herself like that wave becoming and then dissolving.

Once Vincent left the coal field and the north, he ceases to be a preacher and becomes an artist. He finds his voice for colour. She read somewhere that just as there is a tenor voice so there is a tenor's eye or soprano's eye, which would leave the person very sensitive to the visual field. And being overwhelmed was as dangerous as not feeling anything at all. What disturbs her about *Frenzy* is she didn't see it coming. It is as if she has discovered the third woman there amidst Wisdom and Justice. It was Vera who was under the wave; her tongue passing slowly over her lips before she spoke. There she was in Amsterdam. Vera, her cousin, who had died.

She passed through the city in that first spring after the wall came down, on her way to Scandinavia. The only thing that looked the same at the airport, twenty-seven years later, were the iron struts on the ceiling in the oldest part of the original building. But why did she remember it of all things? Perhaps it was the pattern? To people who live a settled existence, nomads are always interesting, because nothing becomes familiarised. It's the familiar which makes us blind.

She had looked at the ceiling the first time, but she didn't see it until the second time she looked. It's like Velcro, she thinks; it comes to meet you. But where do you store the image? And how do you retrieve it purposefully? How do I – focus?

She walks back through the flower market on the hottest summer's day anyone can remember in Amsterdam for years. After Rembrandt Square, she turns towards the canal, and walks between the great narrow merchant houses and the longer houseboats. She thinks again how boundaried Holland is. Time is a respected boundary here, like manners in England.

She brings back some wraps and iced tea to their room. He is surprised that she has returned so soon. He goes off to get a cool beer from the hotel bar. They eat lunch on the balcony overlooking the park. A squad of bicycles have gathered at the side of the young people's residence since morning. The building looks like a Swiss chalet with its half-timbered eaves and wooden structures jutting out over the grass.

I found an Indonesian restaurant near the flower market and I made a booking, she tells him. We can go there this evening. I can use my card. And we need to top up our travel cards, she reminds him. At least I should.

He tells her he didn't manage to do this on the previous evening.

But you went to Centraal Station.

I didn't manage the machines, he says.

She is worried about the extent of the crisis they are facing, but she can't find an opening to discuss it while he is in this panic. It's as if he is so close to her mind that he senses the enormity of her quandary, and he is preventing her from disclosing it.

I want to go to the Red Light District after dinner. I'm told we should wait until it's dusk, she says.

I don't know where that is, he says.

It means going back to Dam Square.

They have sex and sleep until dinner time. She wears a new blue dress, and he takes a photo of her walking onto the balcony. That's your colour, he says. He has taken a good photograph of her and she feels reassured. When she reviews her own images for the day from the flower market she found she has taken one of an empty stand surrounded by peonies and sunflowers. She is pleased about the sunflowers; she didn't notice them when she took the shot. It means she's thinking subliminally about Vincent.

A cameraman once told her when you are in the gate you don't see everything. The eye is a different shape from the lens. And time – we are creatures of time – she thought. We look with the eyes of our time. So why was Vera still hanging around at the edge of the frame?

At dinner she observes they are in a quiet part of the crowded restaurant at the back which they share with an African American couple, and two young women who seem to be on a date. Behind her stands a beatific bronze female deity. I can't seem to get away from stone women, she thinks. She has two glasses of red wine and he has two beers. She wants to find a way of breaking through and telling him how alarmed she is, but they are in too confined a space, and if she can hear the other diners they can overhear her.

They set off for the tram to Dam Square, and this time take the route around to the front of the palace, which seems even more imperial because of the vastness of the space in which it is set. They see that across the breadth of the square there is a troupe of tourists heading off into a side street.

That'll be the way, she says, and they cross the square in a diagonal. Once again, he appears unable to walk at her pace. When did this happen to him, she wonders, as she waits for him to catch up?

They follow other tourists along a cobbled street; the cafés are lit but empty of clientele. There are men standing in the middle of the pavement; she steps around them. He is so far away she seems to be alone, and yet she'd checked he was beside her when they entered the street. A man on a mobile phone steps in front of her and says: how are you? Again, she turns away to look for him and sees that he looks wretched. She stops in front of a window; a woman wearing only black straps of varying widths is standing there in it. Another man steps in beside her to take a photo. She has been warned, no photos in the Red Light District in case anyone thinks you're stalking an errant husband. She walks on to find more deserted cafés, like empty waiting rooms. Porn and the smell of weed everywhere. Wandering about in the dark by the canal, away from the cafés yellow light, and the heat still intense and everything a murmur, it felt Dickensian. There were shadows of people everywhere. The only form of transport appeared to be three-wheeler cycle taxis, ridden around the bridges and streets by the sides of the canal. She thought then this is where the deals are done. Maybe if she hailed one she could get him away to the station again and the tram home before he collapsed.

She wasn't going to give in to the temptations of a wheelchair at the airport the way she'd done on that trip to New York, when they encountered another America. Where women from the ground staff born in Ghana and growing up in St Lucia, women a third of his weight, helped her push the chair. That was seven years ago and since then he had been well. We must be near the station she thinks as she waits for him to reach her.

The Red Light District is always between the port and the station, where we can get our tram back to Leidseplein Square, she tells him.

I need to sit down, he says, soon.

In a side street they press their backs to the wall along with other pedestrians as a four-wheel drive police car passes, the only one she has seen. Her sense of direction is sure as they reach the thoroughfare at the front of Centraal station and the tram terminus. By the light of the tram she sees that his mouth is hanging open, and he appears to be in a state of pained exhaustion and to have difficulty breathing.

Back at the room where they push the door open against a blizzard of frosty air conditioning, they move towards the windows to the balcony and she shows him, from the assembled montage of her day's pictures, the sandstone sculpture of *Frenzy*.

He makes her lift her hair off her face. And he takes a photo. This is you, he says.

No. it's not. We are in this crisis because I am afraid of my own history, she says. Vera is back. She is here in Amsterdam.

Oh, he groans. That old ghost. Will you never let it rest?

I have a photograph. This is from the procession!

It could be anyone. He says, examining the closeup. This is a woman of sixty. When did you last see her? When did she die?

I never saw her again. I told you. She took her own life. When I was starting out for Germany.

There are several coffee pods left in the room for the espresso machine; she makes them both coffee, determined to make him understand.

I have this peculiar gift, she began, in which nothing is real, nothing I haven't dreamt. For instance, you came towards me in a dream before I met you.

He doesn't dare say anything.

I wasn't asleep when this happened, she says. I was waiting at an airport for your flight to touch down; you were coming in from Belfast and I was already in England. The arrivals board said 'Landed'. Ten minutes later you suddenly appeared walking towards me. Then I turned away to get my trolley and you disappeared. You didn't show again for half an hour, and when you did you were walking among a large group of passengers.

What was the difference between me and the ghost?

You were wearing a different shirt. The ghost was wearing the shirt you left at my flat, and I packed it in my suitcase for you, that morning.

He says nothing in reply, but at least she hasn't frightened him.

When I first began to write I lived alone; the gift appeared once I was on my own. I would wake up to neat rows of typing on the ceiling and all would be well. I was simply following the lines. After a while, when I lived with you, the lines faded. I didn't give them much attention anymore. I had a child as well. I went to work for a film company; it was better than writing alone. It was sociable. And it paid well.

When we split up that time, and I found myself sleeping alone again, I'd wake to find to my great relief the lines came back; but this time they were tangled. They ran into each other like a mesh of wires, as if someone had banged the keys on an old typewriter and they all bunched up. It was then I knew the gift that had arrived so mysteriously was damaged.

I often felt because the lines were neat black typescript that I was reading the pages of a book in which my life had already been written. I know now that is a mistake.

She is aware of a certain buoyancy when she closes her eyes, as if carried on a wave again in thirty feet of water. Maybe she has just had too much coffee. She still has not told him how scared she is that the writer, that seraphic witness who sits beside her and wields a pen, will desert her again. Hide around the dark corner, and not turn up on time.

Their days have a structure, so the day of a visit to the Anne Frank House arrives, for which they have tickets. They take the tram again to Dam Square and get off for the third time to catch another at the Rozengracht Junction. They end up right by the canal, where twice in the past few days the barges have stopped. He says he can't wait in the queue; he is unable to stand. She approaches a guide who advises them to come to the side door at the allotted time and someone will let them in. No one comes, so they return to their section of the queue to wait for fifteen minutes and they are let in with everyone else.

The atmosphere changes when she gets into the museum and the well-prepared entrance to the annex behind the bookcase. They climb the stairs to a room which contains a copy of *The Pickwick Papers* in English, open at an extract. England, the desired destination for the exiles who believed they might escape into English. She remembered how she extracted herself from student politics in '69 when the guns appeared, and retreated to the library. The library sailed like a big ship to the safer shores of mind among the books.

They keep climbing in the annex until they are under the roof. It's a kind of nativity this room, she thinks. A writer is born in the rewriting. Anne Frank was editing her diary even as she kept up the daily record. This has been a writer's pilgrimage, after all. Her phone vibrates at her thigh. He is at the exit. I'm in the dairy room, she whispers.

Do you want a coffee here? He asks when she emerges.

I want to get as far away as possible from this building.

It was the postcard from Basel which got me, he admits. They had relatives there.

Somehow, because the legend was so carefully plotted, both orally and on the wall exhibits in the museum, in the heat of the afternoon, in a high-ceilinged room, a faint breeze from the Vondelpark parting the balcony curtains, she dreams of the moment of Anne Frank's capture. She has cast herself as Anne. They are in the street in their finery. She is wearing her good coat and hat. He is also wearing a hat. There is a queue where the uniformed authorities appear to be detaining people; instead of passing by they turn back to avoid scrutiny. For this reason they attract attention. A woman in front of them is stopped, but once her hat is taken she can go. Don't worry, she says, I will remember you. They lose their hats and coats and are held. Before she wakes up, a younger dark-haired woman is helping her to escape from the white wolves, she can hear them howling, by leading her along the narrow streets next to the canal and showing her a place to squeeze into. She finds herself in the kitchen in *The Potato Eaters*. The hull of a boat is scraping through the ice, scrape slide, scrape slide, and the yellow lamp overhangs the table.

It's a dream about money. She tells him the wolf is at the door.

Your problem is, you are a primitive, he says. You mistake manifestations for messages; real messages are information.

I have a savage mind, she says. It's true she would rather deal in omens than in facts.

After Christmas, in January 2017, on the Feast of the Epiphany when she was taking down the tree decorations, she noticed a china dove was missing; she counts to five instead of six. The doves came from a charity shop when her child was three, 27 years ago. Dragging the tree through the narrow door of the house, pine needles scatter. For some reason that year she bought an enormous tree. Her mother couldn't contain her delight. She drops the tree by the side of the house determined to burn it if the binmen don't take it. She returns to the small hallway to find the last white dove still clinging by a thread to a sprig of Norwegian spruce. She picks up the white china bird from the tiled hall floor. The piece held; the bough had broken its fall. They would never know how close it came to being lost. She thinks of him as that white bird, moving off the wall in the photo. But she will never tell him this.

The interior of the big tent in the park has a stripped red and white awning. She settles down at the front row with her feet planted firmly in the woodland floor. Her professional eye picks out several actors embedded among the audience. It's their attire. They seem to be got up as peasants from a Bruegel wedding. Then she notices the Dutch Australian woman sitting opposite, reading her phone. She switches off her own phone and turns her attention to the programme for the play: *Bij De Bron Van De Havik* by W.B. Yeats. Of course, *At The Hawk's Well*. The programme gives her a brief description of the narrative. A young man arrives at the well in search of immortality. An old man is waiting. He has been waiting for fifty years. The well is guarded by a hawk creature who will distract them from their purpose. The hawk is a dancer. She remembers it was a production she attended on her first trip to Holland 27 years before, on her way to somewhere else. It was in the spring after the wall came down. It was staged outdoors amidst modern sculptures in an art gallery. Because of the masks she felt quite distant from it. She wasn't in any mood to tolerate it then, knowing it had its roots in some grand lady's salon. It wasn't her idea of theatre at all.

She finds a name among the cast list which appears in several places: Rose McBride. There's a small programme photo of the woman from the procession. She's sure then the name is made up. She's sure she's found Vera. The resemblance is so striking. It's a good production, and the most dramatic effect is the hawk as a collection of peasants who form a kind of jacquerie in their armed dance, led by Rose McBride. Cuchulain is played by a girl, and the old man is dressed as an old woman in a head scarf; the girl has wasted her life.

At the end, outside in the clearing of another marquee, the Dutch Australian introduces herself as Eva Haas. Have you met Rose?

How's it going? Rose says.

And then the enormity of the moment overtakes her, and she blows it, almost.

I remember you.

They both wait.

You were in the procession with the hares.

Oh, Rose is a one-woman industry.

The three of them walk towards the dressing tent so that Rose can change before they go off for a drink together.

I started out in the theatre myself. My mother and my aunt made costumes for a living. We lived next door to a hall where shows were put on, so they were always busy.

Where was that place? Rose asks.

West Belfast. We left when a bomb went off in the street.

Why would anyone leave a bomb outside your house? Eva asks.

It was 1971, I was 18. There was a feud. Excuse me, what age are you?

The woman in the mirror in front of her has just pulled off a grey and red wig.

I was born in 1973. I'm 44.

Vera would be 70.

Your makeup confused me.

Good, it's my speciality, Rose says. Then she says: we rescue trafficked girls. We do it by disguising their appearance.

Aren't the brothels legal in Amsterdam?

The Dutch woman answers: the brothels are legal, but some of those women are trafficked. Albanians mostly. The regular sex workers have warned us.

Rose butts in and talks over Eva: the brothels are over regulated. It drives some of the workers underground.

She wonders if this failure to recognise generation is a brain injury; another failure of cognitive function. They are seated in a stone-walled courtyard garden of a bar near the park. She suddenly feels hemmed in by the height of the wall; when she glances at the sky it seems a long way off. This is it, she realises, the bottom of the well.

How did it go? Her companion asks when she returns to the room. He is watching BBC World News. A divorce after 44 years is flashed across the screen.

The woman in the photograph of the theatre procession is not Vera.

And did you enjoy the play?

I should have come back sooner, she thinks. Like the youth to the hawk's well, in the spring of 1990 when I first came here. But now it is too late. Everything is too late. She used to think that if she could nail the right word to an emotion she would be free; exorcise that emotion, usually grief in some form, or anger, or a conflict that needs to be let go of. She had recently concluded that she paid a heavy price for naming, and that maybe it was just as effective to foster the emotion out to another place, like Van Gogh's use of colour. Since she painted the hall and stairs in her mother's house, extended her care from the threshold to the attic, it is as if the paint contained a membrane, and she acquired another layer of protection living within it. The house was her yellow submarine.

Nothing was turning out as she'd expected. She believed, rightly or wrongly, and without proof, she had been caught up in a network of control which was not only antagonistic to the whole idea of her autonomy, but it was a state of being from which there never was any exit. All she had was a choice between two deaths; life was never on offer. She would sit there and look at the sky, where a tiny patch of blue was available at the top of a wall while the light held, where an old ghost had entered a stranger. Every word was being weighted.

Why did you return to Belfast to live in your mother's house? Eva probed.

Illness.

She has an image of Van Gogh's *Almond Blossom*, San Rémy, February 1890, like so many white birds on bare branches waiting to alight. She had never been at home in the place where she was born; her passions were released by the latitude of exile. Books were the prosthetic limbs since she came home again to her native, foreign city.

Something had happened. Even knowing the whole story in advance did nothing to change her awareness, because her knowledge was parcelled out to so many different places. Even without the details, the baggage of history, at the age of seventeen she had withdrawn from the protest movement; her older cousin followed her to the safety of the library. And yet something from the time of that withdrawal had come for her. So here she was again, fighting an old demon, and in her mind she knows she will continue to fall victim to these crises if she does not attempt a pathway out from the closed world of the past. Unless I find the language to say what I am trapped in, this is the story that will claim me.

My cousin took her own life. You remind me of her. She says flatly to Rose.

So did my mother.

I'm very sorry.

All during the conversation she notices that Rose puts her hair up and takes it down, pulls a wrap around her shoulders and takes it off. She even scratches her upper bare thigh. But more surprisingly the face is never still. In fact she seems to be inhabiting a cast of characters from her life. Until it occurs to her that the woman in front of her is simply reflecting all her own faces, the way skilful actors do. She once had talked so long with a French actress that when they finished the actress spoke English with a Belfast accent to the director's dismay.

I was born when my mother was 16 and brought up by my grandmother, Rose McBride says. I hardly knew my mother. I thought she was my sister. I was sent to a convent to avoid a scandal; not that my grandmother would have tolerated being thought scandalous. The school was by a lake. I loved it.

What was she like, your grandmother? She asks Rose.

Powerful. People came to her for everything. She didn't go to mass. She was one of those republicans who thought the church had betrayed them. But after my sister's death, she was strict. I couldn't look out of my eyes. When I was old enough, I left the convent and came to Holland and stayed. I met this woman when I was researching a play about sex workers, and she persuaded me to be an activist as well.

How did you get into this business, acting? She asks Rose.

I had difficulty as a child, a form of rheumatism which meant I had to exercise my limbs. So I did dance. What about yourself?

Every parish in Belfast had a hall, and every hall had a show: panto, light opera, you name it. My cousin and I joined a circuit of musical theatre. One night in County Down, on tour in a small market town, I was halfway through my routine after the interval curtain up. I was obsessed, it was the first time I'd been given a dance solo. I became aware of the silence following my every movement. I looked out into the middle of the packed, darkened hall, and right in the middle of the aisle the piano player was walking towards me. I have survived worse humiliations than not waiting for the music.

It is the Dutch woman who turns a critical glance on her and says: do you remember why you became ill?

I woke up and didn't recognise the man I'd gone to sleep with.

Poor man, Eva says.

Yes, I thought there was an old man in my room. I didn't see that he had aged.

In the waiting silence that follows this admission, as the two women watch her without looking at her, she understands that she has become someone who only tells the part about themselves. She has forgotten the story about everybody else. She now perceives that the woman she thought was Vera might be very fragile. She was right to be careful.

Do you know why your mother took her own life? She asks Rose.

She got dementia and she wouldn't accept it, I'm told.

That's common, Eva says. She needed to move from one state into the other. Rather than hovering between.

She didn't want to give up her autonomy, Rose says. In that way she was very much like my grandmother.

Perhaps she wanted to live an unhistorical life, and she hadn't been allowed to.

Eva laughs: no one can live an unhistorical life! Call yourself an Irish woman.

When they leave the air-conditioned room and walk to Leidseplein Square, he is close. By the time she reaches the tram stop, there is a greater distance between them. What can she do? She can't adjust the speed of her stride. She unzips the roller bag and places in it an A4 envelope which Eva Haas had left at the hotel reception; it is about the work the women are doing. She will read it on the plane, if she remembers to take it out of the hold luggage. A jazz singer appears on the theatre balcony opposite the tram stop. She is wearing a black and white gingham dress, she has bright red hair. Accompanied by a female cellist, her voice fills the square. A black saxophonist joins the conversation on the balcony with them. Like a final curtain falling on Amsterdam, her companion arrives with the tram as the song ends.

At Schiphol Airport, she finds herself under the pronged ironwork of the ceiling again when she remembers the envelope.

There is no Gate 45, an airport worker explains, finding them lost between two gates. You will need to hurry, Gate 43 is closing.

The flight is packed, but she has reserved him an aisle seat at the front of the plane. Because he is last on and really struggling, she keeps defending his empty seat from other passengers who challenge her claim to it. One man is so resilient that he won't give up the seat until her partner is standing in front of him. He sits down and leans his brow against the back of the seat in front. The air conditioning has packed up; even the stewardess is flushed in the dense airless cabin. Then she opens Eva's envelope.

Neat lines of an old typeface pace evenly across the page:

In the late summer of 1978, I got a call from Johann. It was his girlfriend. She woke up screaming. She did not recognise him, or her own face in the mirror. He looked stricken when he opened the door to me.

She hasn't slept for three days, he said. We need to give her something.

You look as if you need to take something yourself, I said to him.

The young woman he brought into the room was in a truly terrible state. Very, very frightened; shaking from head to foot, and her eyes were roaming about the room. When she caught sight of me, they stopped, became riveted and focussed.

Are you a doctor?

I nodded, even though I was only in the early years of my specialism in psychoanalysis.

Oh, thank God.

Johann left us.

Everyone is acting. Can you get them to stop?

Johann was devastated. He kept saying: I'll do anything to get her better.

I advised him to take her home; or at least to the place where she came from. He explained that her family situation was difficult. They were republicans. And her mother didn't approve of her current relationship. Given the conditions they

were living under at the time, they couldn't look after a sick
young woman. So, I suggested she should have a change of
scene. At least until her panic receded. He borrowed the
money from me to take her away. He drove her from one end
of Europe to the other. They went south. He was of the
opinion that you don't have to go home. That the new self
she'd wrought with him was the one she needed to be in.

She had been distracted by a phantom. She knew who
Eva was. Johann had a sister, an ice blonde with shoulder-
length hair, like their mother who was Dutch. Somehow
with the short black spikey crop and the Aussie accent she
hadn't been recognisable. What they had done was return
to her a piece of mind.

She'd slept most of the journey which took a couple of
days and woke up in a place in the mountains where he
made her get out of the car. The hills were blue and
scented.

Where are we?

Grasse, the centre of the French perfume industry, he
said.

Before they left in September, she remembered hearing
the news: *die Pape ist tod*. And when they arrived at the
little fishing village on the French coast walking in the
early morning to get bread, someone shouted from one
window across to another overhead: *le pape est mort*.

Did you understand that? He asks.

Yes.

The pope is dead. It's the second time. There were two
popes. One died after the other. It happened twice, he said.
These things are going on outside your mind.

It was there in a small yellow apartment two rows back
from the public beach that she came to herself for the first
time. There were Van Gogh reproductions of sunflowers
on the walls, and in that state she opened her eyes and
saw: *snails like squeezed paint tubes travelling up the walls*

towards the writing on the ceiling ... in a book in which nothing is written. Those were her lines, she wrote that.

She hasn't spoken to him since they boarded the flight when she says: you know that oval photograph in the hallway of my grandparents with my father between them as a baby? He nods.

They were mill workers – she worked in flax and he in flour.

All that dust. Must have killed them.

It did, eventually. But in the photo they all wore beautiful clothes. Particularly the baby.

The studio kept the clothes for them to change into, he said.

It's a nativity, she realises, in *The Potato Eaters*; the yellow glow of the lamp falls on the man's ear. The whole story was there from the beginning. Colour and the absence of colour is like speech and the absence of speech; just as it is the presence of loved companions that keeps the mind in focus.

When they land his foot has become inflamed. You are making me responsible for your health, she says. He is falling asleep at his tea. Why did you leave it so long, the nurse asks no one. The toes now bound in a wad of gauze. Van Gogh slips her mind again until she opens a paper bag from the museum, from the first morning of the first day in Amsterdam, to find a new notebook with a cover of *Almond Blossom*; boughs against the sky, the colour of an azure sea, the branches support the weight of a hundred white birds. Maybe one part of her brain is very old, savage, and the other is that of civilisation, history's auscultation. Maybe what she must do is bridge these two states. She wasn't homeless, she lived in her mother's house; her existence wasn't precarious, she lived between two places. That was all. She lived in the flow, between the overhead lines of conductivity and the clang of trams.

THE ADOPTION FEAST

It was late autumn on a day when the waves were higher than the lighthouse at the mouth of the lough that the lost cousin came to see my mother. This herald of new weather was my mother's namesake, which was how we managed to secure the meeting in the first place. For as long as I can remember her anxiety about visitors ricocheted around the house every time a new visit was proposed. And I discovered something recently which is connected to her anxiety; that when a relative came to visit us in my childhood, my heart froze because her heart froze, and I felt it because we thought they had come to take our place.

The cousin who came was fine boned and sleek, like a cat. She was not like the rest of us. We were stocky and bovine. Young Ellie was accompanied by my cousin Peggy. She is my late father's sister's eldest.

I open the door to them underneath a sepia photo of our grandparents holding my father aloft. I am handed a cake, the shape of a brown loaf with waves of thick cream and walnuts adrift in the hollows and crests. It is edged with paper lace in a see-through carton.

This is protestant cake, Peggy says.

How do you account for this cake having a religion? I ask.

It was made on the Shankill where you find the best bakers.

My cousin Peggy looks very like our grandmother on the wall behind us. They share the same round eyes, set far apart. As do I. Peggy and I could be sisters, while my sisters look nothing like me. The new cousin still has not spoken. We usher her into the living room where a gas fire is blazing, and my mother is waiting.

This is Gael's daughter. She is called after you, mammy. I explain. This is Ellie.

How do you do? It's cold, isn't it? I've met you before, haven't I?

I don't know. Am I called after you?

When she speaks, young Ellie, who looks so unlike the rest of us, compounds the difference in an Australian accent. But it is her uncertainty which is so hard to accommodate.

Peggy has taken over the living room seating arrangements and ushers my mother out of her chair and places her next to young Ellie on the sofa. Then she pulls a chair from the end of the table to the sofa for me. You need to talk to this woman. I'll make the tea.

My mother is staring at her empty chair in the middle of the room, clearly baffled at finding herself removed to the sofa, perhaps remembering why she doesn't like visitors. Especially ones who re-arrange her furniture.

When I was still small, my mother returned to work and I was left with Peggy's mother; who wheeled us both from Albert Street in the Lower Falls, along Northumberland Street and onto the Shankill at least once a week to do her messages. My cousin and I took turns in the Tan-Sad which also held the shopping. Tan-Sad was the trade name for the pushchair we fought to get into – the word shone metallic through the green paint where our shoes had worn the colour away. I have a memory of tiredness in the soles of my feet any time I approach the wall at Northumberland Street, which suggests to me Peggy was more often the victor of our skirmishes. The wall which borders the flourmill where my father worked, until dust in his lungs forced him into early retirement, currently hosts a gallery of political murals, divided from each other by two sets of peace gates. As if it is the images that must be kept apart.

You look very like your mother, I say to Ellie.

Do I? I was very young when she died.

In Australia?

Yes.

What year was that?

1974. She says flatly. I remember the nuns were running about and screaming that morning he took me out of school.

Were you happy with the nuns?

I loved them.

Rather you than me. I always got in a ruckas with them, I say.

Sure, you wouldn't be anybody if you didn't, Peggy says robustly, from the kitchen.

We lived in chaos, Ellie says. They provided me with order, instead of my mother's anxiety about money and putting food on the table. And there were no more big scenes. He was a volatile person to be around. I used to sit in the chapel for hours and look at the blue stained glass.

I found Ellie's feeling so scattered over time, I felt it would be impossible to get her to trace the story from the beginning. Peggy and I met her older sister Dora ten years before, to try to get a clear account. Because of the emotion in the room, and the accusations flying back and forth, we had not met up with her again.

The story presented then was this: my father's little sister Gael had emigrated in the '60s to Australia for ten pounds. Then she had written a letter asking someone, the granny, the same one looking down on us from the hallway, could she please come home? I think she needed forty pounds to return. No one answered the letter. Later came word that Gael was dead. We had not actually managed to find out what the cause of death was, though dark accusations were uttered. And anyway no one wished to pursue the matter of why a letter wasn't answered. Which is where Ellie's big sister's questions were headed ten years before when we fell out of communication.

Peggy, who was one of life's deal makers, anxious that we should all mend relations for the next generation, was clearly giving it her best shot. She emerged from the kitchen with a tray and placed it next to the cake. The small feast preparations had been my job; egg and cress sandwiches and sausage rolls, raspberries on the side of polenta cake. I found it strange to have her waitressing, yet it allowed me to concentrate on the lost cousin.

Seamed plump panels of grey light filled the long window on which our attention was focused. The sky held its cloud bolsters, as snow readied to make its long delayed appearance.

Ellie told us that her young mother was sixteen, babysitting at the baker's house where the groom used to meet her. I remember the baker's house; it had a lovely smell of marzipan. It was across the road from the baker's shop; there were always trays of soda farls and sugared doughnuts on the living room table waiting to be taken across the road to the shop. Gael worked there during the day, but on certain nights she babysat to allow the baker's wife to work in the shop. This happened mostly on

Fridays, when accounts had to be settled. And the baker's wife could do sums in her head. The groom only visited the baker's house on nights when Gael was babysitting. He was the youngest son of a family who owned a chain of shops. Though he was ten years senior than Gael, had she cared for such things, she had made a prosperous match. Somehow the sixteen-year-old in bobby socks, a pencil shirt and startling red hair became noticeably plumper. Peggy's mother, nursing three children, was the first to notice. And this is the version everyone so far has accepted.

I have a very clear image of young Gael, and marvel at how Ellie so closely resembles her.

The first round of accusations alleged a young pregnant girl was quickly wed to an older teddy boy, drainpipe trousers with a velvet collar on his coat; married on a side altar on a weekday morning, amidst the daily communicants, so, not any one of us, and no wedding breakfast followed. It was grim. Ellie's big sister raged at us: so you married Gael off and completely ignored what happened next. Ignored her pleading letters, and to make matters worse when he came back with us in 1974, you wouldn't see us!

My mother very robustly rebuffed these allegations ten years before. It was the middle of the big strike, she said, and besides there was an implication that the groom wanted her to take the three children and bring them up.

What are you going to do about Gael's children, he had shouted on the phone, before my mother put it down. We had all agreed when we heard the story first that my mother had made the right decision in 1974 in ending the call and refusing to add Gael's three children to her own. It was very hard though with Ellie sitting in front of us to repeat that rejection.

This time, however, the extreme uncertainty of the storyteller took us in a different direction. Ellie continued:

when her big brother discovered who had made her pregnant, he went to see him and – here Peggy intervened – chased him down the street. Confirming for me that Peggy was in on the new narrative.

Frank, for that was his name, though Ellie never utters it, pleaded that he couldn't marry Gael because he was to be married the very next day to someone else. The wedding reception was being held at Barnett's Park, and the bride's family had put a deposit on a house.

Your father pinned him to a wall, lifted him, I believe –

A foot above the pavement. Peggy added.

And told him to call his wedding off, or else.

I'll marry your wee sister but you have to break it off with the other one, the groom-to-be said, before he ran off. So the next day it was your father who went to the bride's house.

And my mother went as well, Peggy intervened.

The bride-to-be opened the door, Ellie continued. She thought they were delivering a wedding present, so she showed them into the front room. There were gifts of glass and china laid out on the dining table. The bridal dress hung on the back of the door where the dressmaker had just left it, for the creases to fall out. Your father then explained to the bride-to-be that there would be no wedding tomorrow, for the groom was marrying his little sister Gael; as the couple were expecting their first child in the spring. And then a strange thing happened. As the bride repeated your father's words – no wedding tomorrow –– she turned her head to gaze at the wedding dress; it slipped from its hanger onto the floor. It had a hem of blue cornflowers.

Everyone is quiet when Ellie finishes speaking. And I am aware that something was happening in the periphery of my vison; as if I was looking at a creature, swept by a mudslide into a flood that had become clogged with wreckage, found an opening in the brown water, emerged stained at exactly the point where my mother sat on the sofa. I dared not look away or directly as I knew I would lose this vison. I froze and waited for something to happen.

Into this silence Peggy plants the word 'shotgun'.

Of all the gun accusations my father has been associated with, this is the most absurd.

I don't like my father being blamed for this, I say.

No, Peggy said. I see that.

No one will mention the violence of that marriage, not while Ellie is in the room. And because she seems more brittle since she began to tell the story.

I saw her, you know, Ellie said. When we returned the following year after my mother died. I walked in on them in the bedroom at his mother's house. They were sitting on either side of the room, on twin beds, facing each other. He was crying. She was saying nothing.

Interesting his mother facilitated that reunion, Peggy says.

She never married? The jilted bride? I ask.

Of course she did. And had a family. But whether she loved anyone after him is maybe the point. Because he never loved my mother, Ellie said, her voice trembling.

Do you think he was torn between the two women? I ask.

No, Gael was his line on the side. He was always intending to marry the woman with the dress.

Discreetly the mud-caked swimmer vanishes. My mother resumes her accustomed appearance. I am looking at her plainly, but she doesn't speak. So I improvise on her behalf.

You know, I say careful of the detail. I was told my daddy got her away from him the first time. He left a boxing glove on the kitchen table to stop him coming after her when he took Gael out of that house. He brought you all round to live with her mother and father again.

But her husband did come back for her. One day he lured her away with tickets to Australia.

Gael must have looked out across the blitzed wasteland over the backyard wall, slipped with her children back to him.

We couldn't keep her with us, my mother frets. We lived in my mother's house. We were already under pressure to get our own place.

How did he give that woman up so easily, if he always intended to marry her? And don't say it was my father –

I remember my father from that time when I was little. He had taken up reading, it made him very gentle; I cannot say this out loud because the others would be sceptical. He was a boxer after all.

Gael's mother, Ellie says. Referring to the grandmother in the hallway. Gael's mother went to see his mother. And that was that. After the wedding day they went to live in Ealing, to have the baby. He had a sister there. And then they came back to Belfast.

I used to live in Ealing. I tell her.

Peggy, who has been quiet, asks: are you glad you came back?

I wait, and then I realise the question is directed at me.

Am I glad?

I look around the overheated room. I would be ungrateful if I didn't recognise the gift of sanctuary the house offers; but it is the loss of liberty I feel most keenly. A confinement which is only alleviated by the gorse as it climbs across the Cavehill in the spring; or how the winter trees reveal on the slope below us a clear view of the arrivals to the port and the lough shore across to the Down coast. Halloween neon bursts over the Ardoyne evening when I say: the circumstances wouldn't have been of my choosing.

I'm very glad to have you. My mother says, just when I think she is not listening.

What brought you back? Peggy asks.

I was always intending to come back.

And then the clogged wreckage of childhood joins the flow of memory. When I was eight or nine, I would feel so sad when our overseas visitors, my mother's brothers and sisters, were leaving; just as they were kissing you goodbye a row would break out. This was the most disconcerting thing about grown ups, I never knew where that row came from. But I think now from this distance of years that this unspoken anger is in every leave-taking. I think it has nothing to do with us. It's something the visitors can't express where they live, and they want to leave it behind as a reminder, that they leave to make room for us to stay.

I was fifteen when we came back, Ellie says. Where do they live? I want to meet my mother's family. But his relatives were too afraid to disobey him, they wouldn't take me. They just pointed up at the mountain and said: they live there.

I wish we'd been able to get to know you then, Peggy said, look at all the time we've lost.

He kept us hungry, you know. And he had money. It was only when my sister got a Saturday job that we ate.

I remember the morning she died. She had gone to see the doctor, and she came back and lay down. There was a huge cry. My mother held her arms out in front of her. Ellie demonstrates, throwing up her arms like a child waiting to be lifted. Gael cried out her husband's name and fell back in bed.

Ellie seemed all through the visit like someone who might burst into tears at any minute. And I didn't know if she was always in that mode.

Are you with anyone? I ask her.

No. I used to be. But now I won't have children. There won't be anyone to remember me.

Procreation is not addition, it's a substitution, I tell her. I used to know a man who married three times. But he never was a husband.

What are you saying?

Perhaps there was something in your father that he couldn't complete. The man I used to know kept getting divorced without ever having been married.

I am the only divorced person in the room, so they think I am talking about myself. And sometimes it can happen that a woman, even though she has a child, is prevented by her family from being a mother to her own children.

Why? Ellie asks. It was as if she came into a room and then ran into different corners of it.

Something dysfunctional in the past has overwhelmed them.

My mother died when I was little, she didn't fail me, Ellie insists.

And she was sixteen when she gave birth. She didn't have the resources.

Peggy shifts our attention to a photograph on the wall.

You have Ellie's eyes, Peggy says.

It's an old black and white photo from the '80s. I am so skinny even my nose has lost weight.

Who is that? Ellie asks about a framed colour photo on the mantlepiece of my grandmother; she is wearing a cameo broach at the neck of a blue dress and holding a long stemmed glass of water. Seated, she barely glances at the camera.

My mother's mother. It was her house we lived in when we were growing up.

I know you think you aren't a good catholic, Peggy says, but you are. She is standing with her hand on the door knob, and I'm thinking she won't be able to open the door with one hand.

What do you think happens when you die, Peggy?

Your spirit endures, joins up with all the other spirits. In the flow, you know.

I think you end up living with your relatives. We are standing in the hall when I say this.

She looks at me: well you'd better get on with your relatives and make peace with your situation, or you might end up with the ones you don't like. And in the afterlife that place has another name.

Do you think it's a house?

It's more of a big party, she says. And you all see each other clearly and without distortion for the first time, I suppose.

When I think about that day – before the weather changed – I realise my mother spoke only briefly and never referred to it again. It must have felt as if a flood had washed the debris of other people's lives into the rooms of her house, making them for a time uninhabitable. She had forgotten, or perhaps she never knew, that my heart kept pace with her fears, all those years ago. She regarded me among the visitors.

If I believed that the brown-stained woman, surfacing from the flood to occupy my mother on the sofa, implied the emergence of a hidden self that the presence of her namesake called forth, it was not after all an arrival. She fell. In the days and months that followed, she fell and kept on falling.

The memory nurse at the hospital asks her: how many children do you have?

Oh, I don't know. Two?

She looks to me for help.

Five, I say.

That many? My goodness.

How many brothers and sisters?

Oh, twelve, she says. And names every single one of them.

And who is with you today? The nurse asks.

She's my mother. My mother says.

The counting begins when the days of autonomy are at an end. If you ask her what she is counting as she fingers the air like a child reaching for a piano, she will tell you I am counting the things I have done.

We enter the labyrinth of care providers, who climb rapidly in number from one to eight. The day begins at 6.30am, or 4am on a bad day. Her bedroom universe now a sick room; she leaves us an empty chair downstairs in the middle of the living room where she once sat and was first removed by Peggy. In her sassier days she rattles the sides of the bed to be let out; impatiently throwing her legs over the sides like a gymnast who has failed to clear the bar. But she was never to regain her composure or mobility.

Peggy comes to see her in this phase, and issues an invite to her 65th birthday. Ellie is with her again; my brother will be there, she tells me. He would like to meet you.

In the few hours before their visit my mother had been overwhelmed by waves of nausea. She had been in hospital where I found her on her side, face pressed to the mattress, looking like a neglected child. As if she has fallen down a well, she has begun calling out to us: help me, help me, help me.

I'm worried about her quality of life, I tell Peggy.

Sure, you can't know what her quality of life is, Peggy insists.

The woman in the bed has never been one to argue. She believed in things, she stayed quiet to protect herself. This earned her the reputation for passivity among my father's family.

Since the hospital, I spend the days balancing her sleep with pain.

I open the blinds.

Is that snow on the hills?

Yes, it is. But it won't settle.

I am wrong. By afternoon it is snowing a blizzard. I am inside listening to Laurie Anderson's 'O Superman', and Bach on the same tape someone made for me. I happen to glance and catch a mote floating away. The light from the lamp catches it. And it seems as if there is a leak in the room, as if the outside is slipping indoors on the notes of a song.

O love is very long, it is life which is short.

On the eve of the party I engage a sitter. The Somali woman has my name.

She is wearing a blue headscarf, and I want to introduce my mother to her while I am there in case she thinks she is hallucinating. She will forget you are here, I warn the sitter. Don't take it personally, I say. Don't take anything personally.

I am thinking about an incident with the consultant a few weeks before. He was Asian, and she leaned over, rubbed his skin with her finger and remarked: you are a terrific colour. How did you get that colour?

I was born with this colour. He flashes very even white teeth at her.

He's a real glamour boy. She says to me.

Glamour boy?

It's a Belfast expression.

I am not the one who is sick. She's sick herself. My mother tells the doctor.

He doesn't go on with the tests, so great is her cognitive decline since her last visit. He thinks it's torture for her. What is torture is mobility. I can hardly manage the wheelchair and car park. It is to be her last visit out by car – except for the times she travels by ambulance ferried on a trolley by the paramedics. Spending ten hours in A&E after every fall.

Peggy is celebrating her 65th birthday in a hotel they have renamed; everything has been renamed in this city. I can't find the place. Since the seventies all the old roads have been diverted, re-routed, to new wider carriageways, making everything unfamiliar. I handed the Google map on my phone to my companion; unfortunately in the dark car he drops it under the seat. I rage at him, foolishly, unkindly, in the driving rain.

We are very late to the party – the cake has been cut, the speeches are over, but the disco is throwing its lights around to the sound of music. Ellie is there and she is different, not looking like she might burst into tears, but more in control. She introduces her brother, the middle one, who says, as if we have been in a continuous conversation: you know he only gave her three days to prepare for going to Australia. Three days.

He is sitting with his wife and son. Disco lights roam the walls and empty dance floor like searchlights. 'Dancing Queen' is replaced by 'Super Trouper' which I associate with waiting at ferry terminals in the eighties to come home for Christmas. It was the Christmas of the hunger strikes when I made Baked Alaska to distract the little ones from the roaring crowds at the front door, and my mother bursts into tears at the table because she saw the room empty.

Can you talk to my brother? Ellie says. Tell him what you told me.

What did I say?

Sometimes it happens that a woman's family will not let her go.

You tell him.

You should shoot this, Ellie says. Make a video on your phone. And the camera gives me what I do not see at the time. The disco lights have swathed everything in a lurid turquoise, and a line of shadows appear on the wall behind the dancers, like the profile of a city of skyscrapers or a towering line of the dead.

Suddenly Ellie says: I wish I'd been able to go to her funeral. But we were kept away.

Listen Ellie, I say, she found you when you found us.

Behind the dancers now crowding the floor I look again and see a hem of shadows; still, while everything else is moving. I look on and see tomorrow pass.

If there is a difference between the mad and the sane it seems to me it is this: the sane have a variety of stories to tell, whereas the mad have only one. Or rather they tell the same story over and over. Peggy rises from her full table leaving her young ones to their new liaisons. She shepherds us, the elders, to a smaller room for tea and coffee and night caps.

Party pieces, she calls us out.

My father's younger brother now in his seventies, begins a rendition of 'Wild Rover'; everybody joins in the chorus. I had forgotten this tradition; they will go around the room until they coax a song from everyone. In the past I would have a poem, any recitation would do. But my mind is blank. I'll tell a story, I say at my turn.

One day when I was completely alone, living in south-west England (it was the period after the hunger strikes, but I don't say so in this gathering; there are too many different factions) I had just been out to the bins which were kept in the front garden in a little fenced-off area for the four flats. I closed the door and walked along the hall to the kitchen when the doorbell rang. Impossible, I thought. The street was empty, and the garden path was longer than the hall I had just passed along. A stout shadow filled the glass. I walked back and opened the door. A woman with a long black plait asked to read my palm. I refused. When I tried to close the door, her foot was in the hall. Daughter, she said, there is nothing bad in your face. Sure, what would you be afraid of?

If you tell me the future is bad, I'll kill myself. And if it's good I won't do any work. You will rob me one way or another.

I'm a lucky gypsy. You must cross my palm with silver. And I must give you something in exchange. But you can't send me away. She waits to see the effect this has on me and adds: I've just come from your part of the world. The Lammas Fair, in Ballycastle.

I agree to the exchange. When I come back to the door with the silver, she is on her knees in the hall. She opens a bag and draws from it a ribbon length of lace, and takes a pair of scissors and snips the lace. This is your allotted luck. Then she began a litany under her breath which was so fast and so low it was impossible to make out anything she said. Except this: you will live in two countries. Then she folded the lace into my hands and said: it's what is missing from your life. Next time we meet all I've told will have happened. I kept the lace for years and years, until one day I found it at the bottom of my bag, ink stained and knotted. And I realised that everything I had wanted that day had come true. I had work, a new love, and a new baby all within a few years. So I threw the lace away. And I never saw the woman from the Lammas Fair again.

You were right to throw the lace away, Peggy said, as she walked us to the disabled space at the front of the hotel.

There is something in us which belongs to the future; and often a ceremony is only a confirmation of what has already happened. When she goes into hospital again, I am freed from the four-hourly watches minding her pain relief. So I take him away with me, my companion of thirty years, to stay in a house in the woods. On the second night, in a house we have stayed in in spring, we are expecting our young ones, and I have prepared soup. They told us they might arrive between 11.30pm and midnight. But they are travelling several hundred miles from the south to the north. We go out to the back of the house about midnight, because the reception on our phones is better there. The sensor light in the lane comes on when you stand under it. The arc of light gives instant night vision to the secluded wood. The house itself is like a hide, which bird watchers might use to watch migrating flocks on the lough.

It is described by the letting agents as a small hunting lodge. Built around an internal courtyard which gives onto the back lane. Our phones tell us that they only left Dublin at 10.30. So we adjust our expectations. I think it will be more like 1am, my companion says. But we don't go back inside. It had begun to snow. Under the arc light my umbrella triggered white ladders, streaming through the dark as the snow fell in short ribbons. Stretched, unfurled in transit, they collapsed like a folded concertina on reaching the earth. Mesmerized we stayed on watching this abundance.

They will never find us in this snow, my partner says.

My son is having the same conversation with his girl. I send them the postal code which they ask for. But it only directs them to Lough Neagh. All the roads through the village lead to Lough Neagh on this map, but only the third lane leads to this house.

The snow ladders kept us spellbound. We stayed outside for twenty minute stretches of time, as if we could keep them focused on reaching us if only we stayed put by the door in the lane, if only we kept vigil.

The lane plunges off the road for three miles through several farms, and, at one point after the first gate, it approaches a configuration of four closed gates, which when opened can confuse a wary traveller, because the main track disappears when one of the gates is dragged across it. And just as if it looks like the path is lost through a ruined farm's outbuildings, the way is revealed again passing by a running stream down to the curve in the lane where we are waiting in the light.

They will not find us tonight in this snow, my companion says again. You need to drive up onto the road and meet them in the village.

What if they meet me in the lane where we cannot pass each other? If they'd allowed me I'd have driven to the village half an hour ago. They believe in sat nav and Google maps, I tell him.

So we waited and at 1.10am I called the number. I walked up the path to trace a signal.

Are there blue bins at the entrance to the lane? My son's terse voice asks.

My partner says yes.

I say: you have to look for the name of the house. It is down at road level. Not at hedge level. If there isn't a name you are in the wrong lane.

They take my advice. They drive back to the village and return to count the lanes again.

Nearby an owl hoots.

I ring again. We are in the lane, they say.

Soon the headlights curve towards us amid the trailing ticker tape, and we cheer.

Please go inside and wait, the girl says, as if we are witnessing something private.

Thank you for cheering when we arrived, we had such a struggle to get here, my son says.

The self unfurls on a journey; light reels of snow fall. Pieces of lace I say. Pieces of lace. I dip my umbrella away from the arc light, and the reel ends fade into the night.

Leabharlanna Poiblí Chathair Baile Átha Cliath
Dublin City Public Libraries

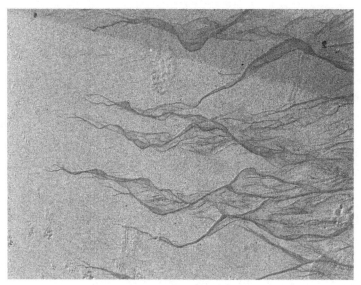

Birds drawn by water rivulets
source: Barbara Mutschler-Hild
photo by author

Acknowledgments

Thanks to the Arts Council of Northern Ireland for granting me a Major Individual Artists Award which allowed me the time to complete this collection of short stories; I am deeply grateful to Dr Damian Smyth for his continuous support and encouragement. I also owe a huge debt of gratitude to Alan Hayes at Arlen House who worked so hard and remained so steadfast in his commitment.

Heartfelt thanks are also due to the following:
Sinéad Gleeson who created two important outlets for my return to short fiction which allowed 'Winter Journey (The Apparitions)' and 'Cornucopia' into print to kickstart this collection; the playwright Winsome Pinnock from the Royal Court days invited me back to read from work in progress at the University of Kingston; Heather Larmour at BBC Radio 4 Northern Ireland commissioned the broadcast version of 'The Transit'; I am indebted to Patricia Craig for reading and editing some of the later work and for her continuing support; Anne Tannahill who so rigorously set me challenges; Gerry Dawe for his critical reading and support; Éilís Ní Dhuibhne for being so inclusive and appreciative of my new fiction; Edna Longley and Michael Longley for their enduring inspiration; Medbh McGuckian for her perspicacity; Carol Tweedale Bardon and her late husband Jonathan Bardon for amazing hospitality and vivid conversation.

The vivid conversation of friends also belongs with some painters: my thanks to Jeffrey Morgan, Graham Jingles, Catherine McWilliams, and Patricia Doherty. Also, thanks are due to Ruth Robinson, Tom Hadden, Ruth Carr, Christine Cozzens, Linda Anderson, Rosemary Jenkinson, Jean Bleakney, Maria McManus, and Tony Kennedy, along with my agents Alan Brodie and Sarah McNair.

The Librarians at the McClay Library will never know how much I missed that library during lockdown, both as a source of erudition and a space of great tranquillity; huge thanks to them. I would also like to thank Julie Andrews and the librarians at the Linen Hall Library; and the Belfast Central Library librarians.

When I lived in Birmingham in the eighties, the Birmingham Writers Lunch was chaired by David Lodge, at a Chinese restaurant in the city, in the company of Stephen Bill, Jim Crace and David Edgar. I miss them all; as I miss Mary Lodge who died recently. When I moved to London in the mid-nineties, Writers Night at the Royal Court Theatre was initiated by Graham Whybrow; my thanks to him, and Caryl Churchill.

Thanks to Catherine Dunne, Lia Mills and Evelyn Conlon in Dublin; Belinda McKeown, Yvonne Brewster in New York; David Clare in Limerick. To Sophia Hillan, Marianne Elliott, Katy Radford, Brice Dixon, Patricia Mallon, Tim Attwood, Chris Reynolds, Paul Arthur, Eileen Weir and the Civil Rights Commemoration Committee 50 years, I owe huge thanks.

My family are owed more than thanks for their love and support: especially my dear sister Moya who died recently, a year after my mother, Theresa. They were both in my care, but we were mutually dependant. Thanks are also due to my sister Patricia Strong and my brothers Joe Devlin and Peter Devlin who made our relocation from London to Belfast so hospitable, along with my paternal cousin Martin Brennan. Thank you to Gerry McMullan, John McMullan, Patricia McAuley, Karen Carlin, Theresa Cunningham.

This book of stories is dedicated to my husband Chris Parr, and my son Connal Parr and his wife Kyra Hild, for everything that makes a life worth living.

May 2022, Belfast

About the Author

Anne Devlin is a short story writer, playwright and screen writer. In the 1980s she wrote *Ourselves Alone* for the Royal Court Theatre; she followed this play in the 1990s with *After Easter* for the Royal Shakespeare Company.

Her prize-winning original work for screen, *Naming the Names*, was based on her own short story from her first collection, *The Waypaver* (Faber, 1986), while her original screenplay, *The Venus de Milo Instead*, was directed by Danny Boyle for BBC Northern Ireland. Her film adaptations include *Wuthering Heights* for Paramount Pictures and *Titanic Town* for BBC Films.

Since her return from London in 2007 she had written a major radio play, *The Forgotten*, for BBC Radio 4, broadcast in January 2009; the BBC also commissioned one of the stories in this collection in 2017. She has recently begun to write essays, and since spring 2020 as Literary Editor of *Fortnight* she has contributed to its pages.

The Apparitions is her second book of short stories.